GEARED FOR ROMANCE

"At least Brian knows who you are," Laura said.

"Yeah," Casey said. "But I get so nervous around Brian, I can hardly talk at all."

"You just need to see him more, get to know him better so you can relax around him," Laura said. "I've got an idea—what about the bike trip to Oak Creek Canyon."

"I don't know what you're talking about. What bike trip?"

"Every year the school sponsors a bike trip the last weekend before school starts. This year Brian is going to help lead the group."

Casey let out a loud groan. "You've got to be out of your mind. I haven't ridden a bike since I was ten years old."

Laura shrugged. "What difference does that make? It would give you and Brian something to talk about, wouldn't it? Of course, if you aren't interested in spending four days with him—" She grinned mischievously.

Bantam Sweet Dreams Romances
Ask your bookseller for the books you have missed

Geared for Romance

Shan Finney

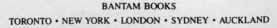

BANTAM BOOKS

TORONTO · NEW YORK · LONDON · SYDNEY · AUCKLAND

RL 6, IL age 11 and up

GEARED FOR ROMANCE
A Bantam Book / August 1988

*Sweet Dreams and its associated logo are registered
trademarks of Bantam Books, Inc. Registered in U.S.
Patent and Trademark Office and elsewhere.*

Cover photo by Pat Hill.

ISBN 0-553-26902-X

Published simultaneously in the United States and Canada

*Bantam Books are published by Bantam Books, Inc. Its
trademark, consisting of the words "Bantam Books" and
the portrayal of a rooster, is Registered in U.S. Patent and
Trademark Office and in other countries. Marca Regis-
trada. Bantam Books, Inc., 666 Fifth Avenue, New York,
New York 10103.*

Printed and bound in Great Britain by
Cox & Wyman Ltd., Reading

Geared for Romance

Chapter One

A pretty girl in a red bathing suit stepped onto the diving board. She took three long, graceful steps, bounced up, and arched into a perfect jackknife dive.

Casey Meadows watched from the edge of the pool, where she and her best friend, Laura Everitt, sat dangling their feet in the cool water. The diver soared for a moment, then sliced downward, entering the water so smoothly that it barely rippled. When the diver kicked to the surface, Casey saw that it was Leslie Duncan, her high school's head cheerleader.

"Leslie's a really good diver," she said.

"It's not surprising," Laura replied. "She's good at everything. You'd be good, too, if you worked at it the way she does."

"Not me," Casey said. "Sports are definitely

1

not my thing. Besides, the best part about summer is that you don't *have* to work."

She stretched lazily and splashed water on her back and shoulders. Casey couldn't imagine wanting anything badly enough to work on it during the whole summer. She thought that some kids were just too serious, and were crazy to spend all their time during the school year chasing after grades or boys, or worrying about which college to attend. Then when summer came, they had to find something else to worry about, instead of enjoying themselves, and most of the time it was a lot of fuss about nothing.

It wasn't that Casey was lazy. She kept up a B average and sang in the school chorus. She just wasn't ambitious. There was enough going on during the school year. The only thing she wanted to work on over the summer vacation was her tan.

"Let's get a soda and stretch out in the sun," Casey said.

Laura nodded and scrambled to her feet. The girls worked their way through a throng of people to get to the line at the snack bar. It was mid-July, the hottest time of the year in Arizona, and both the pool and the snack bar were packed.

Casey was perspiring and very thirsty by

2

the time her turn came at the window. She bought a soda with lots of ice, then turned away from the snack bar to look at the crowd while Laura waited for an ice cream cone. Suddenly her eyes widened.

"Whoa," she said. "Laura, I think I see Brian Warner. Tell me I'm not dreaming."

"Where?" Laura asked.

Without taking her eyes away from him, Casey pointed to a tall, blond boy on the opposite side of the pool. He stood in the shallow water, holding a little girl who was stretched out flat on her stomach. The girl lifted her dripping face from the water and grinned broadly. The boy laughed, and Casey couldn't help smiling.

"Where?" she heard Laura asking again.

"Over there," she said. "The one in the yellow bathing suit, with the little girl in pink."

Laura searched the jammed swimming pool in the direction Casey had pointed, then turned and stared at her. "Wow, you're right," she said. "I wonder what he's doing here."

"I don't know," Casey said. "But I'm not complaining."

Seeing Brian at her neighborhood swimming pool was too good to be true. She had been wild about him since she had first noticed him in her political science class the second semester of the last year.

"He looks good with a tan," Laura said.

"You mean great," Casey murmured.

Although Brian was tall, handsome, and athletic, it wasn't his looks that made him so special to Casey. Nor was it the fact that he had been the smartest student in Mr. Ledderman's political science class. What impressed Casey was how he went out of his way to be friendly with everyone. One day when she was walking to class, he had come up to her in the hall and tried to talk to her about their assignment. Unfortunately, political science wasn't one of Casey's best subjects.

"Did you get that reading on El Salvador done?" Brian had asked.

Just having him speak to her made Casey so rattled that she could hardly think. "Yeah," she had said, trying not to blush.

"This stuff is really wild," he had said. "You never know who's really in power down there."

Casey had barely gotten through the reading, so she didn't really understand what he was talking about. "Yeah," she had said again. She had tried to think of a way to change the subject before he saw how dumb she was. But all she could think about was

Brian walking beside her. It had made her so nervous that her mind went blank.

Her silence had seemed to make him uncomfortable, too. "Guess I'm starting to sound like Ledderman," he had said. "Just what the world needs, huh? Another poli-sci nut!"

You're not at all like Mr. Ledderman, Casey had wanted to say. Instead, she had smiled awkwardly and shook her head. Then the bell had rung and they had to rush into the classroom.

After that, she had studied harder in an effort to impress Brian. But it hadn't done any good. In fact, he didn't even try to talk to her about political science again. The next time he came up to her in the hall, he had said, "You sing in the chorus, don't you?"

The question had taken Casey by surprise. "Yeah," she had replied. "How did you know?"

Brian had grinned. "I have my sources. Being able to sing must be great. I can't even sing 'Happy Birthday' without clearing the room." He had put his fingers against his throat and sung, "Mi, mi, mi," in a high, raspy voice.

It had made Casey giggle. He was good at so many things that not being able to sing couldn't really be that important to him, she had thought. He was probably just trying to be nice. He *was* nice. Before she had thought of anything else to say the bell had rung and it was too late.

Casey had begun thinking about Brian all the time after that. She had watched him in the halls at school and in the cafeteria. Casey had even imagined conversations with Brian, but she hadn't been able to bring herself to approach him.

"Do you think he'll remember me?" she asked Laura.

Laura licked a drip from her ice cream cone and nodded. "Why shouldn't he?" she asked. "Let's go over and talk to him."

Casey hesitated. They couldn't go wading into the water with a soda and an ice cream cone. Besides, just walking up to him was too obvious. He might not even recognize her. "Maybe later," she said. "Right now, I want to get some more sun."

For the rest of the afternoon Casey couldn't think of anything but Brian Warner. Everyone at the pool seemed to know him. Each time she made up her mind to go over and say "hi," someone else got there first. At last, she saw him walking toward the sun deck where she and Laura were lying on their beach towels. Watching him out of the corner of her eye, she sat up and casually combed her fingers through her dark, curly hair. As he was about to walk past her, she waved and called, "Hi, Brian."

Brian stopped and turned around. "Hi," he said, smiling as he saw her.

When Casey saw his smile she nearly melted. Then a curious expression came over his face, and she felt embarrassed. He was probably trying to remember her name. "I'm Casey Meadows," she said. "From poli-sci class, last semester."

"Sure," Brian said. "Casey."

"And this is my friend Laura Everitt. Laura, this is Brian Warner."

"Hi, Laura. Nice to meet you. Hey, Casey, I never got a chance to tell you that that report you did on the Philippines for your final exam was dynamite. I hope Ledderman gave you an A on it."

He sounded so enthusiastic that Casey felt herself blushing. The report had gone okay, but she would hardly have called it "dynamite." "B-plus," she said.

Brian shook his head. "You were robbed."

Casey shrugged, thinking she had been lucky to get a B-plus. "I haven't seen you here before. Do you come often?"

"This is my first time. I've always used the pool at Foothill Junior College. But my family just moved to a new house, so now this is closer."

That's great, Casey thought. But as usual when she spoke to Brian, she couldn't say what she was thinking. "How come you moved?" she asked instead. It was dumb, she thought, just sitting there asking him questions. But it was better than nothing at all.

"We needed a bigger house," he answered. "My sisters were always fighting over the bathroom. What about you? Have you lived in Glendale Heights long?"

"Only forever," said Casey.

Brian grinned. "Then you probably have your own shower. Is that where you learned to sing?"

"No," Casey said. She pretended to be absorbed in smoothing out the edge of her towel. She was flattered that he remembered she sang in the chorus, she just couldn't meet his eyes.

"Really?" Brian asked. "They say it makes your voice sound better. Like being in an echo chamber. Maybe that's what *I* need." He spread one hand over his chest and started to sing in a deep voice.

Casey giggled. "I think you need a little more practice."

Brian pretended to look shocked. "How can you say that?" He grinned and sat down on the deck. "Seriously, though, I have this fantasy that one day I'll just walk into a room and start singing like Paul McCartney, and everyone will stare at me and applaud."

Casey was so flustered that she hardly heard what he had said. He was sitting right next to her, and she couldn't even carry on a decent conversation with him! "Chorus isn't exactly like the Beatles," she forced herself to begin.

The words were barely out of her mouth when she heard someone calling Brian's name. She looked up and saw Leslie Duncan walking toward them.

"Hi," Leslie said, sitting down next to Brian.

"Hi, Les," Brian said. "Hey, I hear you're going to be on the swim team next year."

Leslie leaned back on her elbows, looking slim and gorgeous with her dark tan and red swimsuit. "Yeah," she said. "If I can fit it in between cheerleading and diving practice."

"The team could really use you," said Brian. "But it does sound like you have a pretty heavy schedule."

"Yeah, but no worse than what you do, with football practice and swim team. I figure if you can do it, so can I."

"Whoa," Brian said with a grin. "We're on the same team, remember? Save the competitive spirit for other schools."

"I was only kidding," Leslie said, smiling back

at him. "Really, the team is what I wanted to talk to you about. Now that you live near this pool, we can work on our diving together this summer."

"Sure," Brian said. "I can use all the help I can get."

Casey had been trying to think of some way to get back into the conversation. But the relaxed way in which Leslie talked to Brian made her feel more tongue-tied than ever. She knew she would never be able to talk to him with Leslie around. Perfect girls like Leslie intimidated Casey.

"So can I," she heard Leslie say. "If you have some time now, maybe you could look at my back dive."

Casey's heart sank. She felt Brian glance over at her, but she was too frustrated to return the look. Instead, she started cleaning her sunglasses, hoping he wouldn't notice how upset she was. After a moment he looked away.

"Okay," he told Leslie. "I'll check you out."

"Great," Leslie said, leaping to her feet.

Brian turned back to Casey and smiled. "See you around," he said. "Nice to know we're in the same neighborhood now."

"Yeah," Casey said, forcing herself to return his smile. "Good luck with the diving."

She watched them walk to the diving board and start to work. Seeing them together made her feel more hopeless than ever. Brian practically lived for sports. Leslie was a fabulous athlete and Northside High's head cheerleader. The two of them had so much in common that they didn't have to try to think of anything to say to each other.

They even looked right together. Seeing Brian with Leslie made Casey feel like a troll.

She turned to Laura and grimaced. "Leslie's just too much," she said. "I don't have a chance with someone like her around."

"At least he knows who you are," Laura said.

"Yeah," Casey said. *Me and a couple of hundred other kids,* she thought.

Laura sat up and reached for a bottle of sunscreen. "Why don't you forget about Leslie?"

"It's not just Leslie," Casey said grimly. "It's me. I get so nervous around Brian, I can hardly talk at all."

"You just need to see him more, get to know him better so you can relax around him," Laura said. "I've got an idea—What about Friday night?"

"What about it?"

"The pool party, remember? Now that Brian lives here in Glendale Heights he'll probably be there."

11

"Sure. And so will Leslie. I can't face it," said Casey, looking at the ground.

"Come on," Laura said. "What have you got to lose?"

Casey thought about it for a minute. "Nothing, I guess. Okay, I'll go. But I don't think it's going to do any good."

"Maybe you'll have fun, anyway," Laura said. "And if it doesn't work out, there's always the bike trip to Oak Creek Canyon. I heard Brian is one of the senior counselors."

"I don't know what you're talking about. What bike trip?"

"Every year the school sponsors a bike trip the last weekend before school starts. This year Brian is going to help lead the group."

Casey let out a loud groan. "You've got to be out of your mind. I haven't ridden a bike since I was ten years old."

Laura shrugged. "What difference does that make? It would give you and Brian something to talk about, wouldn't it? Of course, if you aren't interested in spending four days with him, *minus* Leslie—" She grinned mischievously and handed Casey her sunscreen. "Here. Help me with this on my back."

Casey took one look at Laura's pink shoulders and winced. Her own skin never burned, and her face was smooth and golden under her short, dark hair. But Laura, with her fair skin and auburn hair, had to be careful about getting too much sun. She had already stayed out too long, sticking around while Casey tried to talk to Brian.

Now Laura was beginning to burn, and Leslie Duncan was monopolizing Brian. There was no point in hanging around the pool any longer. "We'd better get going," Casey said. "Or else you're going to end up looking like a lobster."

Laura drove Casey to her house. "Think about the bike trip," she said as Casey jumped out of the yellow Volkswagen and waved goodbye.

"Don't be ridiculous," Casey called over her shoulder. "I don't even have a bike."

Actually, she did have a bike, she remembered a moment later as she jogged up the sidewalk and stuck her key into the front door lock. But it was a kid's bike, with fat tires and no gearshift. The last time she had looked at it was probably five or six years before.

Casey changed into a T-shirt and shorts and went into the kitchen. She opened a diet soda and sat down to think about Brian Warner.

Maybe Laura was right. She just needed to get to know Brian better to be able to relax around him. She already knew he was devastatingly handsome, smart, and nice. But she didn't know what his interests were or what he did in his spare time. Now that he lived nearer to her, she would have a chance to find out. At least, she would if Leslie Duncan gave her a chance to get near him.

She thought about the bike trip Laura had mentioned—four whole days with Brian while Leslie stayed behind. A few minutes later, Casey was in the garage moving a stack of paint cans that had been piled in front of her old bike.

The bike seemed incredibly tiny when she finally wheeled it out into the light. The frame and the chrome parts were dull and rust covered, but the tires weren't as flat as she had expected.

Looking at the bike made her think about how small she had been. She wondered if she could still ride it. She pumped up the tires and pushed it out to the front sidewalk. She stood straddling the frame. Refusing to think about how silly she must look, she began pedaling toward the end of the block. She eased the bike over the curb, made a wide turn in the street, and rode back to the house. Although the frame was too short for her now, at least she knew she hadn't forgotten how to ride. But riding up the block and back was nothing compared to a serious bicycle trip.

The whole idea of her going on the trip seemed preposterous, but at the same time it did sound exciting. Laura had said they would be riding in Oak Creek Canyon. Oak Creek was about two hundred miles away, and everyone said it was beautiful. Spending a long weekend there with Brian could be a dream come true.

The more Casey thought about it, the less preposterous it seemed. At least it wouldn't hurt to find out more about the trip. She lowered the kickstand on the bike and dashed into the house to look up the phone number for North-side High's summer recreation program. It wasn't quite five o'clock yet, and the office might still be open. She dialed the number, then waited impatiently while it rang. At last someone answered.

"Can you tell me about the bike trip in Oak Creek Canyon?" she asked. She grabbed a pencil and started jotting down information. The trip was the last weekend in August—a little more than six weeks away. Six weeks was forever to wait to be with Brian. But on the other hand, it didn't give her much time to get ready for the trip. She would have to have a touring bike, a safety helmet, and a sleeping bag, the woman on the phone had said. But Casey knew that the hardest part would be getting in shape and learning to ride well. Why hadn't she spent the summer swimming instead of sitting in the sun?

Maybe the whole thing was crazy, she told herself. There had to be an easier way to get to know Brian. Maybe she could start practicing diving, like Leslie. But diving was even harder than biking. Compared to Leslie, she would be a klutzy beginner. Riding a bike wasn't such a big deal, she decided. She would talk to her parents about the trip when they came home from work.

Chapter Two

That night Casey told her parents about the trip as they were sitting at the round oak table in the dining room, eating homemade ice cream with fresh peaches. The dessert was Mr. Meadows's favorite, and Casey had sliced the peaches at the last minute, hoping it would put him in a good mood.

"It sounds like fun," Mr. Meadows said.

"I think so, too," Casey's mother agreed. "But I wonder, why the sudden interest in sports?"

Casey gave a casual shrug and tried not to blush. If her parents knew the real reason she wanted to go on the trip, they would probably tell her she couldn't go.

"I feel like doing something different," she said. "I've never been anywhere, except on family vacations."

Her father raised an eyebrow. "I assume there will be some adults along," he said.

"Mr. Ramsey and Ms. Williams," Casey responded quickly. "Ms. Williams was my gym teacher last year."

"Sounds reasonable to me," her mother said. "Dave?"

Mr. Meadows scooped up the last peach slice from his bowl and nodded. "It's okay with me," he said. "But we haven't talked about how Casey's going to pay for it. You said there's a hundred-dollar fee for the trip, and you'll have to buy a bicycle and some other things. It sounds as though it's going to end up costing at least three hundred dollars."

Casey's mouth fell open in surprise. She had expected to have problems with the trip, but it hadn't occurred to her that money would be one of them. "How *I'm* going to pay for it!" she exclaimed. "I thought you could just give me the money."

"I wish we could, Casey," Mrs. Meadows said. "But we don't have much money to spare right now. Besides it's *your* trip."

Casey's heart sank. She stared down at her empty dessert bowl to hide her disappointment. She had been foolish to get her hopes up before thinking about how much the trip would cost, and three hundred dollars was a lot of money.

It wasn't her parents' fault that they couldn't afford it.

"I don't see how I can get the money in time for the trip," was all Casey could finally manage to say.

"Maybe you could earn it," Mrs. Meadows said. "You could get a job for the rest of the summer."

Casey grimaced. "No way. Summertime is for taking it easy, not working," she said. "I'd rather not go."

On Friday night Laura came by at about eight to pick up Casey for the pool party. Casey was quiet in the car; she was willing herself to stop thinking about Brian. He might not even be there.

The party was in full swing when the girls arrived. A band was playing on the sun deck, and the lawn was filled with kids dancing barefoot in the grass.

"There's Greg Kelly," Laura said, pointing at a dark-haired boy standing near the refreshment table. "I think he's kind of interesting."

" 'Kind of interesting'?" Casey said as an echo. "Since when? Why didn't you tell me?"

Laura grinned. "It seemed dull compared to the way you've been carrying on about Brian Warner. Besides, who said I liked him? I just said I think he's interesting." Then, without another word, Laura made her way toward Greg. With a shrug, Casey followed.

Greg and Laura were already laughing together by the time Casey made her way through the crowd. "You two have met, haven't you?" Laura asked.

"Not only have we met," Greg answered, "we both suffered through algebra together."

Casey rolled her eyes, remembering the one class she had gotten a C in. Greg had sat across from her; he was definitely a nice guy.

The three of them began filling their plates with barbecued ribs and potato salad. Before they had reached the end of the table, Greg's friend, Ron Bradford, had caught up with them. Greg introduced everyone, and they found a space on the lawn and all four sat down together. Casey could see why Laura liked Greg— he put everyone at ease. Unfortunately, she couldn't say the same for Ron. She had only known him an hour and already he had boasted about his new compact disc player, his scoring average in basketball, and the front-row tickets he had gotten to a Springsteen concert.

"You ought to see the hot set of wheels I just bought," he was saying now.

Greg nodded. "It's a real beauty."

Ron turned to Casey. "I'll take you for a spin when the band shuts down. What do you say?"

"Thanks," said Casey, "but I'm not really into fast cars."

"This baby is *turbo* charged," Ron persisted. "One ride and you'll be hooked forever."

"Yeah," Casey said. "Do you mind if we talk about something else?" She knew she sounded rude, but she was having horrible visions of a never-ending car ride with Ron.

"Fine," he said quickly. "Who was the National League batting champion in 1969?"

"Who cares?" Laura muttered. "I wasn't even born then."

"Come on, take a stab at it, Casey. You're the one who wanted to change the subject."

"John Lennon," she answered, saying the first ridiculous thing that came into her head in the hope of discouraging him.

"Not bad," Ron shot back. "The answer is Pete Rose, but at least the Beatles are in the right era. What was Ringo Starr's real name?"

Casey groaned silently, thinking the party was as awful as she had feared it would be. She hadn't even gotten near Brian. She'd caught a glimpse of him playing water volleyball in the pool, but he had disappeared when the game ended. She never should have let Laura talk her into coming. "If Ringo Starr wanted anybody to remember his real name," she said sarcastically, "he wouldn't have changed it to begin with."

Ron stared at her for a moment, then changed his tactics. "Did I tell you I started bench pressing?" he asked. "I'm up to—"

"Hey, Kelly!" a familiar voice said interrupting Ron. They turned to see Brian, who had just come up behind them. "Where've you been?" he asked Greg. "I haven't seen you since school ended."

"That's what you get for being such a jock," Greg replied with a grin. "Hey, do you know everyone here?"

"Yeah," Brian said, smiling straight at Casey.

Ron stuck his hand out. "You're on the debate team, aren't you?" Brian asked him.

"That's me," Ron replied. "Twenty-two straight wins for Northside."

"That's because nobody else can get a word in," Laura added.

Casey laughed, wishing she had said it herself. Now that Brian was nearby she was suddenly tongue-tied again. Desperately, she tried to think of something, anything, to say. Brian made it unnecessary. He held out his hand to her and asked, "Do you want to dance?"

"Sure." Casey reached for his hand, and he pulled her to her feet. They walked to the end of the lawn where it wasn't so crowded and waited for the next song to start. Casey heard the first quiet notes from the guitar and realized it was going to be a slow dance. Before she could worry about what she was going to do, Brian's arm was around her waist.

He was such a good dancer that Casey actually forgot to be nervous. "Are you getting used to your new house?" she asked.

"Yeah. I like it a lot better than the old one. I think I like the neighborhood better, too." He pulled her a little closer as he said it. All at once, there didn't seem to be any need to talk. She looked up into his eyes and thought what a beautiful shade of green they were. His hair was still damp and tousled from swimming, and his skin smelled slightly of chlorine in the warm night air. Their bare feet touched now and then as they danced in the grass. Before she knew it, the song was over, and Casey felt as though it had hardly begun.

Brian held her for a moment after the music stopped, and she hoped he was waiting for the next song to begin. When the band started up again, he dropped his arm from her waist and stood holding her hand. "I'm not very good at the fast ones," he said. "Maybe we'd better sit this one out."

"Okay," Casey said. She wasn't a great fast

dancer, either, but she was disappointed that the dance had ended so quickly. Then she realized that he still hadn't let go of her hand.

"You know, I didn't want to move," Brian said. "But it's okay. I mean, I don't feel like the new kid on the block, the way I thought I would."

"That's probably because so many kids from Northside live around here," Casey said.

"Yeah," he said. "Especially . . ." He broke off without finishing the sentence and let go of her hand.

Casey looked up and saw Leslie Duncan walking toward them. "Hi, Casey," Leslie said. She turned to Brian with an electric smile. "You play a wicked net, Warner."

"What net?" Casey asked, feeling dumb.

"Volleyball," Leslie explained. "Brian's team totaled us. But we'll beat you next time."

Brian shrugged. "Does it matter who wins?"

"Winning always matters," Leslie answered with a laugh.

He shook his head, and his reply made Casey's heart sink. "Maybe next time we'll play on the same side."

Casey heard the band's lead singer announce the last dance and tried not to sigh. For a few minutes she had felt really close to Brian, but he had let go of her hand as soon as he had seen Leslie. One moment he acted as if he liked her, and the next he didn't seem interested. Casey didn't know what to make of it. But one thing was certain: whenever Leslie showed up, everything started to go wrong. As long as Leslie was around, Casey would never know how Brian really felt. She wouldn't even be able to talk to him. Maybe the bike trip was the only answer.

The next morning after breakfast Casey started the dishwasher and went into the living room to find her parents. "I think I've changed my mind," she said. "Could you help me figure out how to pay for the bike trip?"

By the time Laura called a half hour later, Casey's parents had helped her list all the places in the neighborhood where she might find a job. "Guess what," Casey said. "I decided to go on the trip."

Laura let out a squeal from the other end of the phone line. "Let's go and look at bikes tomorrow," she said.

"Wait till I tell you the rest," Casey said. "My folks say I have to earn all the money to pay for it myself."

"Oh, no," Laura groaned. "You mean you're getting a job?"

"Yeah."

"Incredible," Laura said. "I can't believe it."

Laura's teasing made Casey feel defensive. "Lots of kids work during the summer," she said.

"Sure, but they're not Casey Meadows. You must have totally flipped over Brian Warner."

Casey felt herself blushing. "It was *your* idea," she said. "Besides, it isn't just because of Brian. I feel like doing something different for a change."

"Sure," Laura said as though she meant just the opposite.

"Anyway, I really want to go, and that means I have to start looking for a job on Monday."

Laura gave an exaggerated sigh. "Okay, okay," she said. "If you insist on job hunting, I might as well go along for moral support."

Casey felt a wave of relief and gratitude. The thought of actually applying for a job made her a little nervous, and having Laura along would at least make it fun.

On Monday morning Casey was up and dressed before her parents left for work. "What do people wear to go job hunting?" she asked as she sat down at the breakfast table.

Mr. Meadows put some bread in the toaster and gave his wife a questioning look. "I think what you're wearing is fine," Mrs. Meadows said.

Casey looked down at her white cotton pants and pink-and-white striped shirt. "Are you sure?" she asked doubtfully.

Her mother nodded and smiled reassuringly. "Try to relax, dear. I've never seen you quite so worked up over anything."

Maybe I've never had anything to get worked up about, Casey thought. Her parents would never understand if she told them about Brian. She wasn't so sure she understood it herself. It wasn't as if she had never gone out with boys before. It was just that none of them were as special as Brian Warner.

"You look nice," Laura said when she came to pick Casey up. "Your hair is different."

"It's a mess," Casey said ruefully. "I'm afraid I'm not cut out for job hunting."

Laura shifted the Volkswagen into first gear and said, "This is definitely not the Casey Meadows I know. Where do you want to go first?"

By three o'clock they had been to all six of the places on Casey's list. After Casey left the personnel office at Goldman's Department Store, she went to look for Laura in the junior department. She found her in front of a three-way mirror, modeling a light blue jumpsuit.

"It's you," Casey said. "You should buy it."

Laura looked up with a start, then she saw Casey and smiled. "Maybe I will," she said. "They have it in that pink you like, too. Do you want to try it?"

Casey started to say sure, then stopped herself. She had exactly twenty-two dollars and forty cents, and her allowance was barely enough for swimming and movies. The way things looked right then, she was going to need every penny she could save for the bike trip. "I don't think so," she said casually. "I don't really need it."

"What does that have to do with anything?" Laura asked. She opened the top button of the jumpsuit and tried turning up the collar. Then she saw Casey's face reflected in the mirror and turned around with a sympathetic look. "You were in there for ages," she said. "I thought for sure they were hiring you."

Casey shook her head and shrugged. She tried not to sound too disappointed. "The same old story: 'We have all the help we need right now, but you're welcome to fill out an application.' "

"Don't look so discouraged," Laura said. "This is only your first day at it."

"I know," Casey said. "I just didn't know it was going to be so hard. Do you think it's too late to go to the pool?"

Laura glanced at her watch and nodded. "Yeah, it's getting late," she said. "Let's go to my house instead and listen to records."

"Okay," Casey said. "Don't you want to buy the jumpsuit first?"

Laura grinned. "I don't think so. I don't really need it, either."

Casey knew Laura was just saying that to make her feel better. In a way, it did make her feel better, but it also made her feel guilty. "What does *that* have to do with anything?" she said teasingly. "Just because I can't afford it, doesn't mean you can't. Besides, if you get it, I can borrow it from you."

Laura looked in the mirror one more time. "Okay," she said at last. "I'll get it and put it on my dad's credit card."

Watching Laura charge the jumpsuit gave Casey a new idea. She was sure to find a job soon, but she needed a bike right then. Maybe her folks would let her charge it and pay for it after she got a job.

That evening Casey was still thinking about using a credit card when her parents came home from work. She set the table and went back into the kitchen where her mother and father were fixing dinner together. Her dad pulled a stool up to the counter next to her and started slicing cucumbers and tomatoes for a salad. "Well, how did the job hunting go?" he asked. "Any luck?"

Casey shook her head. "Nobody needs any

help. They all said I should have applied earlier in the summer."

Her dad's forehead wrinkled up the way it always did when he was worrying or thinking. "I was afraid that might happen. I guess we'll have to take a look at the want ads in the newspaper."

"That didn't even occur to me," said Casey with relief. "Maybe there's still hope."

But earning enough to buy a bike was going to take time, and she needed to start training right then. "I've been thinking," she said. "Why couldn't we buy my bike with one of your credit cards? I could pay for it after I get a job. I only need a couple of hundred dollars."

The kitchen became so quiet that Casey thought she could hear the potatoes baking.

"You don't have a job yet, Casey," her dad finally replied. "Give it a week, then we'll talk about it again."

Casey knew she shouldn't be disappointed, but she couldn't help groaning. Her mother stood wiping her hands with a paper towel and said, "Until yesterday, you hadn't even thought about riding a bike in years. One week can't be all that long now, can it?"

"I guess not," Casey said. Seven days seemed like seven years. She started to think about Brian. She wanted to be able to tell him she was going on the trip. Then they'd have something to talk about besides political science class—until he asked what kind of bike she had. Casey would feel silly saying she didn't have one yet. He might think she was just flirting with him the way Leslie Duncan did.

At the thought of Leslie, Casey grimaced. There was no way she could tell Brian she was going on the trip before she actually had a bike. Until then, she would just have to be quiet and let Leslie upstage her.

Chapter Three

Tuesday morning when Casey went in for breakfast, her dad was sitting at the table with the newspaper open in front of him. Casey poured a glass of orange juice and went to look over his shoulder. "Hi," she said. "Oh, the want ads."

Mr. Meadows nodded and pulled a chair over next to his. "Sit down here, and we'll look together."

Casey fixed a bowl of cereal and then sat down next to her dad. She read a column headed "Part-Time and Temporary." It wouldn't take very long, she decided. The entire column contained no more than a dozen ads. Casey was through reading them before she finished eating her cereal.

"Do you think I could be a cashier in a self-service gas station?" she asked.

Casey waited while he read the ad. "I'm afraid not," he said, after a moment. "They want someone to work from eight to midnight."

"I don't mind," Casey said. "I don't have to get up in the morning for school."

"That's not the point," her father said. "I don't think it's a good idea for you to be alone at night in a change booth."

"But, Dad," Casey protested, "there isn't anything else. It's the only job listed here that I *might* be able to do."

"I know, honey," he said sympathetically. "But don't worry. There are new ads every day. Finding a job takes time."

Casey stared at the floor, willing herself not to be discouraged. "I guess I'll just have to keep looking."

"If I had to find a job in another bank, it might take months," her dad said. "We'll probably find something for you in the next few days."

An hour later the phone rang, and Casey jumped up to answer it. "Hi," she heard Laura say. "Can you go to the pool today?"

"Sure," Casey said. "But what about your sunburn?"

"It's all better," Laura said. "Besides, it's too

33

hot to do anything but swim. It's a hundred degrees already."

"Okay," Casey said with a mock groan. "You've talked me into it."

"As if you needed to be persuaded," Laura shot back. "You're probably dying to get another chance at Mr. Wonderful."

Casey giggled. It was true that she was hoping to see Brian again, but she always got embarrassed when Laura teased her about him. She had to remind herself that there was nothing wrong with liking him. "What time do you want to go?" she asked, changing the subject.

"Half an hour," Laura said. "I'll pick you up."

Casey barely had time to change into her swimsuit and get her things together before she heard Laura honking. Now that it was the middle of the summer, she was more grateful than ever that Laura had a car. The pool was near the center of their subdivision, about a mile and a half from Casey's house. Walking there in the July heat seemed to take forever.

The pool was filling up when Casey and Laura arrived. After they had spread out their towels in a shady spot, Casey looked around for Brian, but she didn't see him or anyone else she knew.

"Would you mind helping me with my sunscreen?" Laura asked.

Casey applied a thick layer of lotion to Laura's back. While she was doing it she thought about the bike trip and what bad shape she was in. "I think I'll swim a few laps," she said.

Laura looked at her as if she were crazy. "Incredible," she said and shook her head.

"I know," Casey said, "but I have to get in shape if I'm going to do some serious biking." She plunged into the shallow end of the pool. Before Casey knew it she had touched the opposite end and was turning around to swim another lap. Swimming wasn't as hard as she had expected. Maybe she was in better shape than she had thought, she decided.

She swam two more laps, then pulled herself out at the deep end and looked around. The pool was full, but Brian was still nowhere in sight. At least Leslie Duncan wasn't there either. There was no way Casey could compete with Leslie in the water.

She had been better at swimming than she had expected, Casey mused, so maybe she wouldn't be bad at diving, either. Anyway, there was no one around who mattered to see her if she made a fool of herself. She balanced at the edge of the pool and hesitated, trying to get up her nerve. Finally, she pointed her arms above her head, took a deep breath, and dove in.

A few seconds later she kicked to the surface and swam to the edge of the pool. From the way she had hit the water, she was sure she must have looked like a frog. The entire front of her body stung from slapping the water, and her eyes were burning from the chlorine.

When she finally stopped blinking, a pair of legs appeared just above her. She looked up and saw they belonged to Brian Warner. Why did he have to appear at the exact instant she decided to do a belly flop?

"Hi, Casey," he said. "I didn't know you were a diver."

"I'm not," Casey said, her cheeks burning with embarrassment. "Obviously."

Standing above her, Brian looked about fifteen feet tall. He looked down and smiled. "You just need to get a little more spring and learn to keep your feet together," he said. "Do you want to try it from the board?"

Casey was dumbfounded. She wanted to be with Brian, but she didn't want to make a fool of herself. Reluctantly, she pulled herself out of the pool. She was barely on her feet when she saw Leslie walking toward them.

"Hi, Brian. Hi, Casey."

Casey tried not to groan.

"Hi," Brian said. "I was just offering to give Casey a diving lesson."

"Oh," Leslie said, looking at Casey. "I didn't know you were a diver."

Casey wasn't sure whether Leslie was being catty or just trying to be friendly. "I'm not," she said for the second time. There was absolutely no way she was going to practice diving in front of Leslie. "Thanks for the offer," she said to Brian. "But I think I'll swim a few more laps instead."

Without stopping to think, she dove awkwardly into the pool and began to swim toward the opposite end. She was so embarrassed by the clumsy dive that she swam four more laps before she climbed out and went to flop down beside Laura.

"You're amazing," Laura said. "All you think about is Brian Warner, then when he finally shows up, you take off as though you're training for the Olympics. I thought you hated to swim."

"I did, but not as much as some other things I can think of," Casey said, nodding her head toward the diving board where Leslie stood smiling brightly at Brian.

"I don't think he likes her very much," Laura said. "You just give up too easily."

"Well, what am I *supposed* to do? Every time she shows up I feel like I turn into a great big nothing."

Laura shrugged. "There's still the bike trip."

"*Sure,*" Casey said. "If I find a job. At the rate

things are going, the trip will probably be over before I even get a bike."

"You're taking it all too seriously," Laura said. "Listen, I have to drive my mom to the garage to pick up her car. I'll be back in fifteen minutes."

"Never mind," Casey said. "I might as well go home. There's no point in hanging around here."

"Oh, cheer up," Laura admonished. "I'm getting tired of watching you mope around. You need to get your mind off Brian. How about a movie tonight?"

Casey sighed and then grinned at her friend. "Okay, I'll go with you tonight—and I promise not to mope!"

"Look who's here," Laura said as she and Casey walked into the lobby of the Festival Theater.

Casey turned to see Greg and Ron in line at the snack bar. "You really like Greg, don't you?"

Laura grinned. "He's sweet, don't you think? Come on, let's go get a soda."

Casey trailed along reluctantly. She could tell Laura was glad to see Greg. She knew she should have been happy about it, but she couldn't help wishing that Ron wasn't there, too. He had been a real bore at the pool party. Now she was afraid of getting stuck with him again. At the same time, she was afraid she hadn't been a very good friend to Laura lately. The least she could do now was to stop being so preoccupied with her own problems and help Laura get together with Greg.

The boys saw them coming and waved. "Hi," said Greg. "Since we're already in line, tell me what you want, and we'll get it for you."

"Cokes," Laura said, tugging a couple of dollars out of the pocket of her jeans.

"I'll get it," Greg said, waving away the money. Laura smiled and gave him a questioning look. "No, really," he said. "I insist."

Casey sighed. This was beginning to look more like a date every minute. For a second she wondered if Laura had planned it without telling her.

"That was a great party the other night," Ron said. "I couldn't have done it better myself."

"Yeah," Casey said. "It was okay." Dancing with Brian had been the only really good thing about the party as far as Casey was concerned. That, and seeing Laura and Greg having fun together. The time she had spent with Ron had certainly not been a high point.

"We'd better go in," Laura said, grabbing Casey's arm. She flashed a smile at Greg. "See you around."

"Okay." Then Greg grinned and said, "Hey, wait!"

Laura gave Casey a meaningful look and walked over to speak to Greg. "Save me a seat. I'll be there in a minute," she said.

Casey nodded and went into the theater. A few minutes later Laura squeezed in beside her. "What did he want?" Casey whispered.

"They asked us to go for an ice cream after the show."

Casey grimaced in the dark. Running into Ron and chatting with him was one thing, but going out for ice cream with him was something else. It was just too much like a date.

But the girls had come to the movie in Laura's car. If Casey insisted on going home right after the show, Laura would have to leave, too. Considering everything Laura had been doing for her lately—listening to her problems, helping her find ways to see Brian, driving her around to look for jobs—Casey decided she would put up with Ron. Keeping Laura from being with Greg just wouldn't be fair.

"All right," she said at last. "I'll go—but just this once. And I'm only doing it for you."

Chapter Four

The next Friday morning Casey was lying in bed thinking. When she had asked her parents to let her charge a bicycle, her dad had said to wait a week and see what happened. Since then she had read the want ads every day and called about every job that seemed even remotely possible. She always heard the same story: "The job is already filled," or, "We need someone with experience." The second excuse was the most frustrating. How were you supposed to get experience when nobody would hire you?

Casey sighed and climbed out of bed. Getting a job was as difficult as getting five minutes alone with Brian. He had been at the pool every day the past week, and he always came over to talk to her. But they were never alone together long before Leslie showed up.

41

Leslie was obviously flirting with him, but at the same time she always had a legitimate reason for needing Brian's attention. "I can't get any speed on my backstroke," she had said the day before. The day before that, it had been, "Brian, my back dive still needs work."

Thinking about it made Casey cringe. Leslie and Brian had so much in common that anything Casey had to say to him seemed unimportant. All she wanted was to get to know him better, and she wasn't good at flirting. Her tongue would suddenly seem to be tied in knots; she always ended up standing around feeling helpless and watching them walk away together.

The worst part was that she could never figure out how Brian felt about her. Every time Casey saw him, she felt Brian seemed to like being with her, but then Leslie would show up and everything would change. Sometimes Brian seemed embarrassed about it, but he never actually objected to Leslie's attentiveness. Either he liked Leslie or he was just such a nice guy that he couldn't say no to her.

Casey figured she would never know which was true until she was sure she was going on the bike trip. Once she had the trip to talk about she'd be able to hold up her end of a conversation. Brian might spend more time with her instead of with Leslie then.

But the trip was just about five weeks away, and she was no closer to getting a job or buying a bike than she had been a week before. Maybe now her dad would let her charge the bike.

She found her dad in the kitchen clearing away the breakfast dishes. "Hi, Dad," she said. "Remember what you said about waiting to see what developed?"

Mr. Meadows nodded and opened the dishwasher. He seemed more hurried than usual, and Casey had the feeling he wasn't really listening. "Well," she said, "if I don't get a bike soon, I won't have time to practice for the trip."

Mr. Meadows turned around and smiled, but he seemed distracted. Just then, Mrs. Meadows came in with her purse over her shoulder. "Good morning, Casey," she said. "Are you ready to go, Dave?"

"Almost," Mr. Meadows said. He turned to Casey. "Sweetheart, I have a lot on my mind right now, and I'm going to be late for an early meeting at the bank. Can we talk about this tonight?"

"Sure," Casey said. Her father was normally so calm that his tense expression made her wonder if something was wrong. She wanted to give him a reassuring hug, but she could see that he was in a hurry.

After her parents left, Casey worried about her dad's anxious look. It probably didn't mean anything except that he was late for his meeting, she told herself.

She was worrying about everything lately, and it was getting her nowhere. It was time to start having fun again, she resolved. A little while later Laura called and asked her to go shopping. Casey agreed instantly. Soon, she and Laura were at the village mall, looking in windows.

"Let's go in here," Laura said, pausing in front of a shop that sold funky clothes. "I need something different to wear for my date with Greg tomorrow night."

"Okay," Casey said.

"By the way," she added casually, "I think Ron Bradford's going to call and ask you to double. I wish you'd come."

Casey considered it. It might be fun to double with Greg and Laura, but she couldn't stand Ron Bradford. "I don't think so," she said. "It just wouldn't seem right."

She followed Laura into the shop and helped her pick out half a dozen outfits to try on. Finally Laura bought a cotton striped shirt and a red miniskirt, and they window-shopped through the mall until they came to Selby's bike shop. Casey paused and glanced in the window.

"We might as well look," Laura said, starting into the shop.

Casey wrinkled her nose skeptically. She had been in a bike shop earlier in the week, and she had learned a lot. A very patient salesman had spent a lot of time answering Casey's questions and offering her advice. He had shown her several different bicycles and given her a bunch of brochures to take home to study. The most important thing she had learned was that the only two models she really wanted—a silver Cameron Toro or a red Mitchel Le Tour—cost close to three hundred dollars.

"There's not much point," she said. "I can't afford to buy one yet, anyway."

"Maybe they'll have some cheaper ones," Laura said. A moment later she was inside the shop, reading the price tag on a blue ten-speed. "This one is only a hundred and seventy," she said.

Casey walked over to look at the bike. "I don't know," she said in a minute. "It has steel wheel rims."

Laura pretended to look horrified. "Oh, no! I wouldn't be caught dead with steel wheel rims," she gasped.

Casey felt defensive again, but she couldn't help laughing. Being picky about a bike when she had twenty dollars to her name did seem silly. In the past week, though, she had learned there were certain features that were necessary to have in a touring bike. *Not* having them wasn't much better than having no bike at all.

"It's not just the way it looks," she explained. "The brakes press against the wheel rims. If steel rims get wet, you need five times longer to stop. Aluminum rims are safer."

"Incredible," Laura said. "Mr. Halsey would be impressed."

Casey grinned. Mr. Halsey had been their physical science teacher last year. Casey had barely pulled a B in his class. "It's not the same," she said. "Physical science didn't have anything to do with anything."

"You mean it didn't have anything to do with Brian Warner," Laura said.

"That's not what I said," Casey protested amiably. It *was* incredible how much she had learned about bikes in so little time. Then again, just because she had never been ambitious about her studies, didn't mean she was dumb. Figuring out how a bike worked wasn't the same as studying the speed of light.

"Actually," she told Laura, "bikes are kind of interesting, once you begin to understand how they work."

"I guess I'm not that interested," Laura said. "Do you think your dad is going to let you charge one?"

Casey remembered her father's face and the way he and her mother had rushed off that morning. "I don't know," she said. "But something tells me this isn't a good time to ask."

When Mr. and Mrs. Meadows came home from work that night, Casey had already set the table and started making a salad. "Thanks for starting dinner," Mrs. Meadows said. "It's been a long day."

Casey knew that both of her parents had difficult jobs. Her mother was a customer service representative for an appliance company, and she spent most of her day solving problems for clients. Mr. Meadows had his own share of problems as the supervisor of the loan department at the Glendale Heights branch of the First Southwest Bank.

But neither of her parents usually came home complaining that it had been a long day. Casey figured it had to do with the way they had acted that morning and decided to wait until they were ready to tell her about it.

She was still waiting by the time they started dessert. "Okay, I think somebody should tell me what's going on. I'm part of this family, too," Casey said.

Mr. and Mrs. Meadows looked at each other the way they always did when Casey knew something she wasn't supposed to know. "What makes you think anything is going on?" Mrs. Meadows asked.

"You and Dad," Casey said. "You aren't acting normally."

Her mother smiled and started to say something, then her dad interrupted. "She's right, Betty. This is a family matter." He put down his fork and looked at Casey. "Honey, there's a lot going on at the office right now. This is a tough time for the banking business, and a lot of people are being laid off."

Casey remembered him saying it could take him months to find another job, and a lump formed in her throat. She swallowed hard to get her last bite of cake down. "Does that mean you could lose your job, too?"

Mr. Meadows looked thoughtful. "It's not very likely," he said gently. "But we have to consider the possibility. Right now, I have to decide who we'll keep and who we'll let go. It's not a very pleasant position to be in."

"I'm sorry, Dad," Casey said. "But I'm glad it's that way and not the other way around."

"I guess I am, too," Mr. Meadows said. "But nobody likes putting someone else out of a job." All at once, he seemed to remember something and smiled. "I almost forgot—I have some news for you."

"What?" Casey asked. "Is it about a job?"

Mr. Meadows nodded. "Mr. Howard, who runs the swimming pool, came into the bank today. I told him you were looking for work, and he said he could use some extra help at the snack stand. It seems the pool is especially crowded this year, and he wasn't ready for it. Particularly on weekdays."

Casey couldn't believe her ears. "You mean I could work at the pool?" It was too good to be true. If she got a job at the pool, she could continue seeing Brian while she earned money for the trip.

"It sounds pretty good," her father said. "I told Mr. Howard you'd call him tomorrow. He'll probably ask you to come in for an interview."

Casey's excitement faded instantly. "Oh, no," she groaned. "He probably wants someone with experience. Everyone else does."

"I don't think that will be a problem," Mr. Meadows said. "I told him you haven't worked before."

"All you need to do is make a good impression, and I know you won't have any trouble doing that," Mrs. Meadows added.

"Thanks, Mom. I hope you're right."

"I know she is," Mr. Meadows said, smiling at Casey.

Casey grinned back at him. "I can't believe

it!" She jumped up from the table and reached for the dishes that her mother had started clearing away. "I'll wash up," she said. "You and Dad just relax."

Mrs. Meadows gave her husband a suspicious look. "I've never seen a sixteen-year-old girl quite so happy about getting a job," she said lightly. "Do you suppose there's something going on here that we don't know about?"

"Never look a gift horse in the mouth," Mr. Meadows said. He winked at Casey and folded his napkin on the table.

Casey wondered if her parents knew about Brian. But they couldn't possibly know, could they? She carried a load of dishes into the kitchen quickly, before they had time to ask her about it.

A few minutes later the phone rang. Mr. Meadows answered and told Casey it was Ron Bradford. "Just as I suspected," he said. "There had to be a boy in the picture somewhere."

Casey rolled her eyes and shook her head. "Sorry, Dad, you've got it all wrong. Ron is just a friend of Laura's new boyfriend." She took the phone and said, "Hello."

"Hi," Ron said. "I got your number from Laura. I thought maybe we could double date with her and Greg tomorrow night."

For a moment Casey hesitated. The idea of

Laura dating Greg made her feel a little left out, but she knew that Ron wasn't her type. If she got the job at the pool, she was going to have more important things to do than go out with him. "Thanks for asking me," she said. "But I already have plans."

Chapter Five

Saturday morning Casey could hardly wait until ten o'clock when the pool would open. The hands on the clock seemed to be moving in slow motion. When she wasn't watching them creep forward, she talked to her parents about what she should say to Mr. Howard. At five minutes to ten she got out the slip of paper with his phone number on it and perched on a stool beside the telephone in the kitchen.

"You probably don't have to call him on the stroke of ten," Mrs. Meadows said. "He might need a minute or two to get the office opened."

"But, Mom," Casey said. "Someone else might call him first. I *have* to get this job." At one minute after ten, she dialed the phone. "This is Casey Meadows," she said. "May I please speak to Mr. Howard?"

A few minutes later she hung up the phone and leapt into the air like a cheerleader doing a victory jump. "He wants to see me!" she yelled. "He wants me to come in for an interview at five o'clock!"

By four-thirty that afternoon, Casey was dressed and ready to leave for her appointment. "You're going to be early," Mrs. Meadows said after she had driven Casey and stopped the car outside the pool.

"I don't mind," Casey said. "It's better than being late." A few minutes later when she was waiting outside Mr. Howard's office, she wasn't so sure. The wait seemed to last forever, and Casey was so nervous she could hardly sit still. At last, Mr. Howard came to the door and asked her to come in.

"I guess you've been to the snack stand enough to have a pretty good idea what the job is," he said as he sat down behind his desk.

"You mean selling sodas and hot dogs and things," Casey said.

Mr. Howard nodded. "You'll have to learn to cook the hot dogs and operate the soda machine and cash register. It's not difficult. The hardest thing for most kids seems to be remembering that they're at work. When your friends come up to the window, you can't stop and visit with them. You have to keep the line moving."

He paused and looked at her. Casey smiled and tried to look responsible. "I know I can do it, Mr. Howard," she said firmly.

He kept looking at her, as if he were trying to read her mind. It made Casey uncomfortable, but she remembered what her dad had told her and forced herself to look back at him.

"The hours are noon to four, Monday through Friday," he said at last. "I need someone I can depend on to be there. Precisely at noon. Maybe even a few minutes before."

Mr. Howard was starting to look like an ogre. Casey told herself to ignore it and tried not to blink her eyes. "You can definitely depend on *me,*" she said quickly.

Mr. Howard nodded his head again. "Are you available to start work Monday?" he asked after another long silence.

When Casey heard the question, she felt certain she had the job. She was so excited she almost jumped out of her chair. "Yes," she said. "The sooner the better. Does that mean you're going to hire me?"

Mr. Howard smiled for the first time since Casey had come into his office. Suddenly he no longer resembled a monster. In fact, Casey decided, he seemed to be a very nice man. "Thank you, Mr. Howard," she said, grinning back at him. "I promise not to disappoint you."

"I think you'll do just fine, Casey. Report to the snack stand at noon on Monday. I'll tell one of the regulars to be prepared to show you the ropes."

"Great," Casey said. "I'll be there." She forced herself to walk calmly out of his office, but it was all she could do to keep from jumping up and down. Immediately, she began to calculate just how much money she would earn and what she could buy with it.

Mr. Howard had told her how much the job paid per hour, and that she would get a paycheck every two weeks. It seemed to be a small fortune until she thought about the price of the silver Cameron Toro. All of a sudden, it seemed like nothing.

But, she reasoned as she started home, if she worked the whole five weeks until the trip, she would earn enough to get by, even if she couldn't afford the Toro. Somehow, she would just have to find a cheaper bike. When she did, maybe her dad would even let her charge it.

She was so caught up in her thoughts that she looked up in surprise when she realized she was almost home. In her excitement, she had forgotten that her parents would be out. All of Casey's efforts had finally begun to pay off, and now there was no one with whom to celebrate.

As soon as she got in the house, Casey reached for the phone and dialed Laura's number. "Guess what," she said a moment later. "I got a job!"

"Wow!" Laura said. "Where?"

"You won't believe it," Casey said. "At the swimming pool—working in the snack stand!"

"That's great," Laura said. "I wish you were doubling with us tonight so we could celebrate."

"I know," Casey said. "But I really just don't like Ron. Have fun, though. Greg seems like a great guy."

After she hung up the phone, Casey fixed a sandwich and poured a glass of milk, wishing that Laura could come over and eat with her. She felt left out, knowing that Laura was going out with Greg while she spent Saturday night alone. If Greg and Laura started going together, it would probably happen all the time. Laura had been her best friend for three years. Now, Casey wondered if Greg was going to take her away. Maybe she should have gone to the movies with them, but it was Laura she wanted to see, not Ron Bradford.

Casey wondered what it would have been like

if it had been Brian instead of Ron who had asked her out. The next thing she knew, she was imagining that he had called. She could hear herself saying, "Hi, Brian, what's going on?" After a while, it all started sounding so real that she almost convinced herself that he was actually going to call her.

Even though she knew it was ridiculous, she kept expecting the phone to ring. "Don't be an idiot," she told herself when nothing had happened by nine o'clock. "Nobody calls for a date on Saturday night."

She went to bed early and lay awake, thinking about biking with Brian in Oak Creek Canyon. They were racing down a hill together, going faster and faster. They were both laughing when they finally coasted to a stop alongside a mountain stream. And as they left their bicycles to go for a swim, Brian drew her to him for their first kiss.

The next morning when she woke up, Casey's dream was still with her, and somehow it seemed possible. After all, she had a job. Now all she had to do was persuade her dad to let her charge a bike.

But her parents still hadn't heard the news! Casey jumped out of bed, pulled on a pair of shorts and a T-shirt, and ran to the kitchen.

Mr. Meadows looked up from the newspaper and said, "How did it go, sweetheart?"

"I got the job!" Casey shouted. "Mr. Howard wants me to start work on Monday."

"That's wonderful," Mr. Meadows said. "I'm proud of you, Casey."

"So am I," Mrs. Meadows said.

"But the problem is, I won't get a paycheck for two weeks. Now that I have a job, do you think we could charge my bike?"

Mr. Meadows looked thoughtful. "I'm not sure credit cards are always the best solution," he said after a minute. "Why don't I lend you a hundred dollars?"

"Dad, you can't get anything decent for less than two hundred."

"That's a lot to spend on a bike, sweetheart. Particularly if you consider that your interest in biking is a bit sudden. I'd hate to see you spend the whole summer working for something you may get tired of in a few weeks."

Not likely, Casey thought. At this point, saying she might lose interest in a bike was like saying she was going to lose interest in Brian. She could never explain *that* to her parents.

But her dad interrupted her thoughts. "Let's look at the classified ads and see if we can find a used bike. You might get a better one for a lot less money. Come on, I'll help you look."

Casey was so frustrated that she could hardly stand it. She had imagined herself soaring downhill with Brian on a shiny new Toro. If she had to show up with a beat-up, secondhand bicycle, she might as well forget the whole trip.

She made herself think about Leslie Duncan. If Casey ever wanted to get Brian Warner alone, she *had* to go on the trip.

She sighed and went to look over her dad's shoulder at the newspaper.

"What about this?" he asked. "Pelham ten-speed, seventy-five dollars."

"I guess it could be okay," Casey said reluctantly. "It depends on what model it is."

Mr. Meadows continued reading. "Here's another one with two bikes for sale," he said, after a minute. "A Mitchel for eighty-five dollars and a Cameron for one thirty-five."

"You're kidding!" Casey exclaimed. "The bike I want is a Cameron Toro."

Two hours later Casey climbed into the front seat of her parents' car and gave her dad an exasperated look. They had been to four different places, and Casey couldn't believe the old, rusty, beat-up bikes they had seen. She wouldn't be caught dead riding any of them on a bike trip with Brian.

"This is hopeless," she said. "All we've seen is junk. At this rate I'll never get a bike."

Mr. Meadows looked at the list of addresses they had written down earlier. "Maybe you're right," he said. "But we've only got two places left to go. We might as well check them out."

Casey tried to hide her frustration. "Let's go to the one that had two bikes for sale."

When the man who had advertised the bikes showed them into the garage where they were stored, Casey could hardly conceal her disappointment. The cheaper bike was a model that she had already tried on one of her shopping trips. It looked great, with good paint and clean, shiny chrome, but it wasn't right for the trip to Oak Creek Canyon.

"It's pretty," she said. "But it would be too hard to pedal on long uphills."

The owner seemed to understand. "There's no question this one is a better road bike," he said, wheeling over the Cameron.

"I know," Casey said. "But I can't afford it. I've only got a hundred dollars to spend."

Even though it was out of her price range, she went ahead and examined the bike. The frame looked good, but the brake cables looked dry and cracked, and some of the chrome parts were caked with mud and gunk. "It's a Challenger," she told her dad. "If it wasn't so messed up, it would be almost as good as the Toro."

"It's a top-of-the-line-bike," the owner said. "But I guess it has been neglected. Maybe I can come down on the price."

Casey's eyes lit up. "How much?"

The owner thought for a moment. "Say, a hundred and ten."

Casey looked at the bike again, then turned back to her father. "Let's get it, Dad. I've saved the extra ten dollars from my allowance. This model is a little harder to shift than the Toro, but it's easy to pedal and it's even got aluminum wheel rims."

Mr. Meadows looked surprised at how much Casey knew about bikes. "It sounds as though you've done your homework," he said. "But the bike is going to need work. Have you thought about how you're going to pay for the repairs?"

Casey was desperate. She had to get a bike soon so she could start training for the trip—*and* so she could tell Brian she was going. It seemed as if she had been waiting forever. If she could only spend a hundred dollars, she would never find another bike as good as the Challenger.

"I'll do the work myself," she said. As soon as the words were out, she felt as astonished as her dad looked. She didn't even know how to ride a ten-speed, let alone repair it. But she *had* to have this bike.

All at once she was sure she could find a way to get it in shape. When she thought about spending four days in Oak Creek Canyon with Brian, nothing seemed impossible.

"Do you really think you can handle the repairs?" Mr. Meadows asked.

Casey nodded her head vehemently. "I *have* to," she said. "I could never afford a brand-new bike like this. This model's got great braking and handling, and the paint's almost perfect."

Mr. Meadows looked impressed and doubtful at the same time. "Assuming that you can fix it up," he said, "will you be happy with a boy's bike?"

Casey rolled her eyes in exasperation. "Don't be ridiculous, Dad. It only matters if you're wearing a skirt. *Nobody* rides bikes in a skirt any more."

Mr. Meadows smiled at his daughter and took out his checkbook. A few minutes later they were loading the bike into the car and tying the trunk shut. Back at home, Casey took the bike out for a test ride. The brakes were noisy and sluggish, and the pedals seemed to grab occasionally. There was no question that she would have to work on it before she could start any serious training. But once she got it reconditioned, she was sure it would be just fine.

She wheeled it back into the garage and stood looking at the shiny red paint. At last she had a job and a bike. On Monday she would call the school and sign up for the trip. After that, she could tell Brian, and then, what? She wasn't exactly sure, but she had a feeling things might just start to fall in place.

Chapter Six

Monday morning Casey called the school to sign up for the trip. A deposit was required to secure her place, but they agreed to let her pay it when she got her first paycheck. As soon as she hung up, she phoned Laura to tell her the news. "What time is it?" Laura asked sleepily.

"Almost nine," Casey said. "I thought you'd be up. Or were you out with Greg again last night?"

"No," Laura said, "but we have a date for next weekend. Anyway, what if I was?"

"Nothing," Casey said. "I just wondered why you woke up so late. Guess what—I got a bike."

"That was fast," Laura said. "Did your folks let you charge it?"

"Are you kidding? My dad made me buy a

used one. It's okay though, almost like the one I wanted. The only thing is, it needs some work."

"What kind of work?"

"Nothing serious," Casey said, trying to sound convincing. "I think I'm going to do it myself."

Laura's voice was incredulous. "Are you sure you're feeling okay? You don't even know how to change a light bulb."

"So what?" Casey said. "Bikes don't have light bulbs. Anyway, that's what I called about. Do you want to go to the library with me to look for bike books? I have to start work at the pool at noon."

"Sure," Laura said. "Casey Meadows, girl mechanic. I wouldn't miss it for anything. Besides, I want to see your bike while it's still in one piece."

Casey laughed as though Laura were being ridiculous, but she wasn't as confident as she sounded. It was true she had never done anything like this before. She could still hardly believe she had practically begged her father to let her do it.

She felt as though she were trying to find her way through a maze to Brian Warner. Every time she came a step closer, there was something else she had to do. First her parents had told her she had to earn the money for the trip. Then she finally got a job, and she still couldn't

65

afford to buy a bike. At last, she had a bike, but she couldn't start training until she repaired it.

Suddenly Casey wondered if she was as crazy as Laura seemed to think she was. Instead of taking it easy the way she usually did, she was spending half her summer vacation trying to get ready for a bike trip!

Then she thought about Brian again. Even if she couldn't start training yet, she *could* tell Brian she'd signed up for the trip. Having something to talk to him about was *definitely* not crazy!

Fixing up a bike couldn't be that hard, she told herself firmly. Casey was still telling herself that an hour later when she and Laura drove to the public library to look for books on bicycle repair. On the way over, Casey told Laura about her new job.

"It's going to be weird seeing you working at the pool," Laura said as they walked into the quiet building.

"It won't be so bad," Casey said. "It's only four hours a day. Besides, I'll probably see Brian every day."

They stopped at the card catalog and looked up where to find the books on bicycles. A few minutes later Casey and Laura were sitting on the floor, thumbing through books.

Casey turned a page and felt her forehead

wrinkle in a worried frown. She had almost convinced herself that repairing a bicycle couldn't be all that difficult. Now, she was shocked to see how many parts there were to a bike.

"Sometimes I wonder if it's worth it," she said. "You didn't have to work this hard to get a date with Greg."

"Sure," Laura said. "But Greg isn't exactly the boy of my dreams."

Casey stuck her fingers between the pages she was reading and stared at Laura. "You're kidding," she said. "Then why do you go out with him?"

Laura shrugged. "He's fun. I mean, I like him a lot. It's just that I'm not totally flipped over him the way you are over Brian."

When Casey thought about it, she knew what Laura meant. She had gone out with quite a few boys, but none of them had ever affected her quite the way Brian did. "I guess that's it," she said. "I'm beginning to believe that if you want something special, you just have to work for it."

"You sound like my mom," Laura said, opening another book. "This looks complicated. Do you really think you can repair the bike?"

"Why not?" Casey said, trying to regain her confidence. "Besides, I don't have any choice." She put three books in a stack and returned the others to the shelves. "We'd better get going," she said. "I'm supposed to be at work in half an hour."

"Okay," Laura said. "Aren't you even nervous?"

"A little," Casey said. "I've been so busy thinking about how to fix up my bike, I just haven't had time to worry about my job."

Twenty minutes later when Laura dropped her off at the pool, Casey changed her mind. There was a long line of kids in front of the snack stand window. She took one look at them and started to feel panicky.

"Hey, Casey," she heard someone say. Casey looked up and saw a girl she knew from school named Donna waving at her from inside the window. Casey waved back, and Donna pointed to a door at the side of the snack stand.

After that Casey was so busy that she didn't have time to worry. Donna showed her how to operate the soda machine, scoop ice cream, and wrap hot dogs. Donna did everything with an easy rhythmic motion. She had a small transistor radio tuned to a rock station, and she literally danced around the small stand. Everything about her was so relaxed and friendly that she made the job seem easy.

"You can take a break after the rush," Donna said. "Then I'll show you how to cook hot dogs and work the cash register." She gave Casey a sympathetic look and smiled. "It's not always this busy," she added. "Noon is the worst time."

Casey peered at her around the package of paper cups she was opening and smiled. "That's the best news I've heard all day," she said. Every time she looked up, she saw another face asking for something to eat or drink.

At last the rush was over. Casey saw that no one was left standing in front of the window and gave a sigh of relief. She had been watching for Brian, but he never appeared.

Maybe it was just as well, Casey told herself. She couldn't stop working to talk to her friends, and Brian definitely would be a distraction.

"Do you usually do this all by yourself?" she asked Donna.

"Yeah," Donna said. "It wasn't bad until this month when the pool got crowded. I'm sure glad you're here."

"Me, too," Casey said. "I really needed the job." All of a sudden her stomach grumbled loudly. "Sorry," she said. "I was in such a hurry to get to work that I completely forgot to eat."

Donna smiled and looked at the clock. "It's almost two o'clock," she said. "Why don't you take a break and have a hot dog or something."

Casey hesitated. She was starving, but she was still worried about spending money. Her first paycheck was two weeks away, and she wanted to buy whatever she needed to fix up her bike as soon as she could.

"Go ahead," Donna said. "It's free. That's one of the good things about working here. If you like junk food, that is."

"It's better than nothing, anyway," Casey said. A few minutes later she stood eating a hot dog, trying to spot Brian in the crowded pool. She was about to give up when she saw him walking toward the diving board. He climbed the ladder to the high dive and bounced on the end of the board.

Casey watched while he arced into a perfect swan dive. Now that she could finally tell him she was going on the trip, maybe she'd be able to figure out if he had any feelings for her from his response. But she'd have to wait until she got off work and hope he was still there.

After Casey's break, Donna showed her how to cook the hot dogs, operate the cash register, and make change. The snack stand wasn't nearly so busy as it had been when Casey arrived at noon. She went back to work and handed two sodas through the window, and went to the cash register to make change. When she returned to the window, her heart almost stopped beating. Brian was the next person in line!

"Hi," she said, trying to sound casual.

Brian looked surprised. "Hi, Casey. I didn't know you were working here."

"I just started," Casey said. "It's my first day." Now that she finally had a chance to tell him about going on the trip, she felt so awkward that she could hardly speak to him.

"Well, how do you like it?" Brian asked. "So far, I mean?"

"It's okay," she said. "I need the job to pay for the bike trip to Oak Creek Canyon. I hear you're going as one of the counselors." The words sounded casual even to her, but her stomach felt as though it were tied in knots.

"You're kidding!" Brian said, then he looked embarrassed and smiled. "I mean, I am one of the counselors, but I didn't know you were going on the trip. How long have you been biking?"

It was Casey's turn to feel embarrassed. After the way she had sat like a lump through political science class, Brian must already think she was an idiot. He would think she was a complete fool if she said she had never even ridden a touring bike.

"You should have asked how long I *haven't* been biking," she said, jokingly. "I just decided to take it up again."

Two girls came up behind Brian at the window. Casey glanced at them nervously. She wasn't supposed to talk while people were waiting in line. She didn't want Brian to leave, but she didn't want to lose her job on the first day, either.

Brian seemed to have read her mind. He looked over his shoulder, then turned back to her and smiled. "I guess you're busy," he said. "Do you have strawberry frozen yogurt?"

Casey nodded and smiled back at him, then went to get the yogurt out of the freezer. The way he had smiled made her feel scattered. She was determined to act normally around him, and she was afraid her own smile had been too bright. But she couldn't help it. Something about the shape of his mouth and the warm glow in his green eyes always gave her a tiny thrill.

She found the cup of strawberry yogurt and returned to the window. "It's seventy-five cents," she said.

Brian handed her a dollar bill, and she went to the cash register to make change. "I'm glad you're going on the trip," he said when she came back and handed him his quarter. "It's going to be great."

Brian glanced over his shoulder again. "I'd better let you get back to work," he said. "Talk to you later."

Casey wanted to stand there and watch him walk away, but she forced herself to pay attention to the two girls waiting at the window.

Another group of kids came up behind them, and a line began to form.

While she scooped ice cream and made hot dogs, Casey thought about what Brian had said. He was glad that she was going on the trip, but maybe he said the same thing to everyone. That was the trouble with getting hooked on such a nice guy. She couldn't tell if he was treating her differently from everyone else.

At least they had something to talk about now. When the rush was over, she looked around for him again. After a minute she saw him standing near the deep end of the pool, looking tanned and handsome. Then she saw Leslie Duncan walking toward him and let out a loud groan.

"What's the matter?" Donna asked, alarmed.

"Nothing," Casey said quickly. "I was just thinking about something." *Hadn't* been thinking was more like it, she told herself. She had been so excited about being able to see Brian while she was at work that she had almost forgotten about Leslie. At last she had something to talk to him about, and she was stuck in the snack stand while Leslie hung around flirting with him.

At three-thirty she saw Brian pull on a striped T-shirt and start walking toward the exit gate: her heart sank when she realized he was leaving. Then, as he walked past the snack bar, he stopped and waved at her. Casey leaned out the window and waved back. After that, she felt better. At least he hadn't forgotten she was there. Maybe she was on the right track after all.

That evening when her parents came home from work, Casey was sitting in the dining room studying the library books she had checked out that morning.

"How was your first day at work?" her mother asked.

"It was okay," Casey said, turning a page to examine a gear diagram. She had been so absorbed in learning about her bike that she had almost forgotten about starting work that day. Figuring out how a bike worked was similar to solving a puzzle. Every time she looked at an instruction or diagram, it led to another instruction or diagram.

"Just okay?" her dad asked.

Casey looked up just long enough to see the curious expression on his face. "It's not hard," she said. "And Donna, the girl I work with, is nice."

After dinner she took the library books out to the garage to compare the diagrams with the parts of her bike. Little by little, it all began to make sense. She examined the brake levers on the handlebars and traced the wires that ran from the levers to the rubber pads near the wheels.

There was nothing mysterious about that, Casey decided. Sitting with her back against the wall, she propped the book against her knees and began studying the section on gears.

It was astonishing how quickly she could learn when she set her mind to it. She imagined how the bike would look when she was finished with it and made a mental note to buy solvent and lubricant to clean the gunk out of the chain and wheel spokes.

The next thing she knew, her dad was shaking her by the shoulder. "I think you'd better come in and go to bed," he said.

Casey opened her eyes sleepily, then looked up with a start. "But I'm not done yet," she said, reaching for the book that was still propped on her knees. "What time is it?"

"Nearly eleven o'clock," Mr. Meadows said. "You've accomplished enough for one night."

Chapter Seven

Casey splashed cool water on her face, pulled on red shorts and a tank top, and went to the kitchen to get a glass of orange juice.

"Good morning," Mrs. Meadows said. "I didn't expect to see you up so early this morning."

Casey shrugged and reached for a blueberry muffin. "I need all the time I can get to work on my bike. The trip is just four and a half weeks away." From the way her mother kept looking at her, she knew she was in for a lecture. While she was waiting for it to begin, she took a bite of muffin and chased crumbs around her plate with one finger.

"Don't you think you're overdoing it a bit?" her mother said at last. "Your father and I are both pleased at the way you've taken responsibility for your trip, Casey, but we'd like to see you take some time out for fun, too."

Casey sighed. Her parents had wanted her to get a job and pay for the trip. Now she had only worked one day at her job and fixing the bike, and they thought she was working too hard. "You're the ones who wanted me to get a job and buy a used bike," she said. "Besides, working on my bike *is* fun."

Her parents exchanged looks, and Casey stared down at her plate. Even though no one was talking, she felt as if she were eavesdropping. Sometimes she was fascinated by the way each of her parents could read the other's mind just by looking at each other. That day it gave her the creeps.

Just when she thought she couldn't stand the silence another second, her dad smiled at her and said, "That's a good point. I guess we're just not used to seeing you this way."

Casey grinned back at him. She could understand why her parents thought something was wrong. Even she was amazed at how much she had changed since she had decided to go on the bike trip. "I guess *I'm* not used to it, either," she said. "But the funny thing is, I'm enjoying it. I can't wait to start working on the bike, but I need some tools and things."

"What do you need?" Mrs. Meadows asked.

Casey reeled off the list she had memorized before falling asleep the night before. "Screwdrivers, pliers, a small wrench, and something to dissolve the stuff that's caked in the chain and gears. And I'll have to replace some screws and nuts."

"I think I have the tools you need," Mr. Meadows said. "We can shop for the other things before dinner tonight."

"Thanks," Casey said. "That's just what I was hoping you were going to say."

After her parents left for work, Casey wheeled the bike out of the garage and rode over to Laura's house. There was a squeak in the brakes as she stopped in front of Laura's door, but she couldn't tell for sure whether it was coming from the levers on the handlebars or the brake pads.

Whatever it was, she had to fix it soon. The screech was so loud that Laura opened the door before Casey had time to press the doorbell.

Laura seemed surprised to see her. "I thought you'd be home working on your bike," she said.

"I'm taking it out for a test drive," Casey said.

"Do you have to do it now?" Laura asked. "I was hoping we could go shopping."

"I can't," Casey said. "I have to work on it now, so I can be at the pool by noon."

"I have to go to Goldman's to look for a bathing suit. I'll stop by later, though, and give you a lift to the pool."

As Casey rode back home she tried to visualize the gearshift and how it worked. She wasn't ready yet to try shifting gears. The shift lever was on the column that connected the bike frame to the handlebars. That meant she had to look down and steer with one hand while she reached for it with the other. Both she and the bike were still too shaky for that. Until the bike was fixed up, she could use it as though it were a single-speed.

When she got back to her house, she returned the bike to the garage and began studying the diagrams again.

Laura finally arrived, and there was just enough time to have a soda before Casey had to leave for work. "What did you buy?" she asked.

Laura pulled out a teal blue bathing suit and held it up in front of her.

"I love it," Casey said. "It's perfect with your hair." As glad as she was that she finally had a bike, she missed shopping. For a second she wondered if Brian would notice her more if she bought some new clothes. It didn't matter, because she couldn't afford to buy anything now, anyway. She already owed every paycheck she was going to earn for the next month.

"Do you think Greg will like it?" Laura asked,

tucking the swimsuit back into the Goldman's bag.

"Sure," Casey said. "Are you going swimming with him?"

"Maybe," Laura said. "He's coming over this afternoon. It's almost time for you to go to work. I can drop you off at the pool, then I could come back with him later."

Casey brightened. "Sounds good. You can have one of my gourmet hot dogs."

Later, when Greg and Laura appeared at the snack stand, Casey almost wished they hadn't come. She was stuck in the tiny booth while everyone else was swimming and getting a tan. It had been bad enough when it was only Brian she'd been watching.

He had arrived about an hour ahead of Greg and Laura. Casey had been keeping her fingers crossed, hoping he would still be there when she got off work. She only had an hour to go, but the hands on the clock moved so slowly that she wondered if they had stopped. Then, at last, it was four o'clock.

As she walked out of the snack stand, she saw Greg and Laura talking to Brian at the far end of the pool. For once, Leslie Duncan was on the high dive instead of standing six inches from Brian's elbow.

Brian saw Casey coming toward them and

smiled and waved to her. Casey's heart skipped a beat. It all seemed too good to be true. In fact, it was so perfect that she suspected Greg and Laura must have had something to do with it.

"Hi," she said when she reached the far end of the pool. "What's everybody doing?"

"We were talking about baseball," Greg said. "Brian coaches a summer team for the recreation department."

"You're kidding," Casey said, smiling at Brian. "Is there any sport you don't do?"

Brian laughed, but his eyes looked shy. "I guess not," he said. "It just seems to come naturally. How's the biking?"

Casey gulped and glanced toward the pool as Leslie Duncan split the water in a stunning back dive. "I haven't really got started," she admitted reluctantly. "My bike needs some work."

No matter how hard she tried, things seemed to keep going from bad to worse. Brian was sure to think she was hopeless now that he knew she hadn't even started riding.

But when she looked back at him, he was still smiling. "Most of them usually do," he said. "What kind of bike is it?"

"Challenger," Casey said. "I just got it last weekend."

Brian's eyes lit up. "You must be more into

biking than you're letting on," he said. "The Challenger is one of the best touring bikes around. I wish I could afford one."

"I know what you mean," Casey said. "I bought mine used." Suddenly talking to Brian was easier; she had almost forgotten about being tongue-tied.

"Sounds like it was a lucky find," Brian was saying. "What kind of work does it need?"

"I'm not positive yet," Casey said. "Mostly just cleaning up the rust and gunk, I think. I'm doing it myself."

Casey was surprised when Brian looked thoughtful, instead of laughing at her as everyone else had when she told them she was doing the work herself. "The tough parts are the brakes and gears," he said. "Adjusting the derailleur can be really hard." He hesitated and gave her a questioning look. "Do you know about the derailleur? It's the part that lets the gears shift."

Casey grinned. "That's *all* I know about it," she said. "I still haven't figured out how it works." Just then, she glanced toward the diving board and saw Leslie Duncan starting to walk toward them.

Greg must have seen Leslie at the same moment. "Hey," he said suddenly. "Why don't we all go for a pizza or something? I don't think I can stand to watch Laura devour another ice-cream cone."

Casey cast a suspicious look at Laura. Obviously she had told Greg *everything* and he was trying to help Casey get together with Brian. Casey thought it was nice of him, but she wished he had been a little more subtle. She was afraid Brian would think she was in on it.

"Sure, why not?" she said, trying to sound more nonchalant than she felt. She would have given almost anything to have Brian go for pizza with them. At the same time, she didn't want him to think she was like Leslie Duncan.

Her confusion made her self-conscious again. She could feel Brian looking at her, but she couldn't quite bring herself to look at his eyes. "I wish I could," he said. "But I have to meet with my baseball team in about forty-five minutes."

Casey's heart sank. She smiled to hide her disappointment, then she heard Leslie Duncan say, "Hi, what's up?"

"I was just leaving," Brian said. He turned to Casey and smiled. "Let me know how it's going with your bike. I might be able to give you a few tips if you need them."

"Thanks," Casey said. "I'm probably going to need all the help I can get."

*   *   *

Ten minutes later she was riding home in the backseat of Greg's old car. Seeing Greg and Laura together in the front seat made her feel as though she were a fifth wheel. She thought about Brian and wondered if he really had to meet with his team or if he had only used that as an excuse to get out of going for pizza.

The whole thing was too embarrassing. "Listen, you guys," she said. "I know you were trying to help, but it's not going to work."

Greg glanced over his shoulder and grinned at her. "Hey," he said, "if you expect to get anywhere with the guy, you've got to let him know you're interested."

"Yeah," Laura said. "Why don't you just call him up and ask him to the movies or something? We could double-date."

Casey let out a loud groan. She didn't have any objections to calling a boy before he called her, but she still wasn't sure how Brian felt about Leslie Duncan. Until she had a better idea, she wouldn't call Brian Warner and ask him for a date. "No way," she said. "Maybe some people need more time to get acquainted. Not everybody likes to rush into things."

"Sure," Laura teased. "Like deciding overnight to get a job and become a bike mechanic isn't rushing into anything."

"It's not the same," Casey said, feeling defensive again. She had to admit that Laura was right—in a way. It was true that she had already made up her mind to get to know Brian. In fact, she was devoting her whole life to it. But, somehow, that wasn't the same as calling him for a date.

Besides, everything she was doing wasn't just for Brian. It had started out that way, but now she was beginning to enjoy learning about her bike. Laura just didn't seem to understand that, even though she was her best friend.

It didn't matter, anyway. The one thing Casey knew for sure was that she had to do this her own way. Whether it made sense or not, there was absolutely no way she was going to call Brian and ask him for a date.

Chapter Eight

Friday morning Laura followed Casey out to the garage and stood staring at her bike. "It's incredible!" she said. "It almost looks brand-new."

"Of course," Casey said as if she had never doubted that it would. "What did you expect?"

For the past twelve days, since she had gotten the bike, she had spent all her free time reconditioning it. She had been all thumbs until she got used to handling the tools. After that, it was mostly a matter of taking things apart, cleaning them, and carefully replacing them with new nuts and washers.

Now the Challenger gleamed as though it had just rolled off the showroom floor. Hearing Laura's praise, Casey felt a glow of pride. At the same time she felt more desperate than ever. It was already the end of the first week in August, and the gears weren't shifting properly. With the trip about three weeks away, her bike wasn't ready for Oak Creek Canyon yet.

"It *looks* great," she told Laura. "But Brian was right. Adjusting the derailleur is tough."

"Would you mind translating that into English," Laura said, rolling her eyes at the ceiling.

"The part that lets the gears shift," Casey explained, pointing to the part near the gear cluster on the back wheel. "I can't do any serious training until I get it set right."

"Oh," Laura said. "Maybe Brian knows what to do."

Casey nodded and gave Laura a perplexed look. Since the day Greg and Laura had tried to get her and Brian together for pizza, she had been asking his advice. Brian was an expert on bikes, and he never seemed to mind when she asked for help.

That was just the trouble. At first, she hadn't been able to talk to him at all. Now they talked for a few minutes almost every day at the pool, but all they talked about were bikes.

When she went to work a few hours later, she saw him standing near the snack stand. "Hi," she said. "I'm glad you're here. I've got another problem with my bike."

Brian listened while she described her gear problems. "It sounds like the derailleur, all right," he said. "Maybe I could stop by and take a look at it tomorrow."

All of a sudden Casey's heart was pounding hard. "That would be great," she said, hoping she sounded calmer than she felt.

If he came to her house, they might actually get a chance to talk about something besides bikes. She wondered if Brian was thinking the same thing and ducked her head to hide the blush rising in her cheeks. "I've got to get to work," she said.

Brian smiled, and Casey nearly melted. Then she remembered that he didn't know where she lived. She grinned and shook her head, hoping he wouldn't think she was a complete idiot. "I live over on Magnolia Street," she said. "Wait while I get something to write the address on."

She got a slip of paper from the snack stand and wrote down her name, address, and phone number. "I really appreciate it," she said as she handed him the paper. "I've tried everything, but nothing works."

"It takes awhile to get a feel for it," Brian said. "What if I come by around ten o'clock?"

"Ten is fine," Casey said. "I'll be home all day, anyway." Immediately she wished she hadn't said that. The next day was Saturday, and she didn't want it to sound as if she had nothing to do but wait around for him. "I mean, I don't have to work," she explained. "I planned to spend the day working on my bike."

Brian glanced at the paper she had given him. "Great," he said. "Maybe I can give the whole thing a quick check. See you tomorrow."

For the rest of the afternoon Casey could hardly keep her mind on her work.

At ten minutes to four Mr. Howard came to give her and Donna their paychecks. When she had first started work, two weeks had seemed like such a long time to wait to get paid. Now that payday had arrived, Casey was astonished at how quickly the time had gone by. Between working and trying to get the bike ready, there were never enough hours in the day.

"You're doing a good job," Mr. Howard said as he handed her a white envelope with her name on it. "We're glad to have you aboard."

"Thanks," Casey said. "I'm glad to have the job."

Before she had time to open the envelope, Laura's face appeared in the window of the snack stand. Laura had been spending so much time with Greg lately that Casey was surprised to see her at the pool alone. "Hi," she said. "What are *you* doing here?"

Laura shrugged as though the question didn't deserve an answer. "Don't you want a ride home?" she asked. "I thought maybe we could go to a movie tonight."

"You're kidding," Casey said. "I thought you were going out with Greg."

"I decided to take a break," Laura said. "I can't spend *all* my time with him."

Casey wondered if there was something that Laura wasn't telling her, but she was secretly relieved. Between the bike and her job and Laura spending so much time with Greg, she and Laura hadn't seen much of each other lately. Going to a movie would be a welcome change.

"Guess what," she said as they walked to Laura's car. "Brian's coming over tomorrow to help me with my bike."

"Why do you sound so surprised?" Laura said. "He probably would have done it a long time ago if you had only asked him."

"But I didn't ask him," Casey said. "It was his idea."

"You're hopeless," Laura said, rolling her eyes and grinning.

Casey grinned back, but she wondered why she always felt so defensive when Laura talked about her and Brian. "I got paid today," she said to change the subject. After she got in the car, she opened the white envelope and looked at her check. "Oh, no," she said. "This check is for less than I expected. I forgot they would take some out for taxes and social security."

She looked at the check again. She owed her dad one hundred dollars for the bike. That meant after two full weeks of being stuck in the snack stand, she would barely have anything to show for it. Fortunately, her allowance had covered the bike parts she had bought, but she still had to pay the deposit on the trip fee.

That evening before dinner, Casey showed her parents her check. "It's a good thing we found a used bike," she said, trying not to sound as discouraged as she felt. "I still have to pay the fee for the trip, plus buy a backpack and a safety helmet."

Her parents exchanged one of those looks that always made her suspicious, and she wondered what was coming next.

"Maybe we can arrange some easier terms for repaying your loan," her father said. "Why don't you just pay me fifty dollars now? You can give me the rest when you get your next check."

Casey was so relieved that she threw her arms around his neck and hugged him. "Thanks," she said. "That means I can go ahead and get some things for the trip."

Mrs. Meadows smiled. "I hope it means you're going to buy a safety helmet before you start riding," she said. "How's the bike coming?"

"It's all done, except the gears," Casey said. "A boy from the pool is coming over tomorrow to help me adjust them."

"That's nice," Mrs. Meadows said. "Anyone we know?"

Casey shook her head and hoped they couldn't see her blushing. "Brian Warner," she said. "He's a senior counselor on the trip. He knows everything about bikes."

She tried to make it sound as if he was just another boy. She wasn't sure she wanted her parents to know how she felt about Brian yet.

The next morning she was awake at the crack of dawn. It had been ages since she had slept late on a weekend. She thought about staying in bed, but decided not to. The birds outside her window were making so much noise that she couldn't go back to sleep, anyway.

Mr. Meadows was always the first one up in the house, but that morning when Casey went to the kitchen her dad wasn't there. The dining room curtains were drawn, and the newspaper was still on the front doorstep. The whole place felt deserted.

Casey looked at the clock on the kitchen wall, and it all started to make sense. It was only six-fifteen! She had nearly four hours to kill until Brian came over. Suddenly four hours seemed longer than the entire two weeks she had waited for her first paycheck.

She turned on the television, but there was

nothing to watch but the early news and cartoons. She switched off the set and went out to the garage to look at her bike. Laura had been right—the bike looked as good as new. The chrome and red paint glistened, and even the tires were spotless.

Unfortunately, the area around the bike was a mess. Tools and rags and discarded parts were scattered everywhere. Just looking at them made Casey feel like a slob. She picked up the trash and arranged her tools and extra parts on a shelf. By the time she finished and went back to the kitchen, her dad was there reading the paper.

"Good morning," he said. "Have you had breakfast?"

"Not yet," Casey said. "I've been out cleaning up the garage." She went to the kitchen, fixed a bowl of cereal, and brought it back to the dining room.

"What time is your friend coming over?" Mr. Meadows asked.

Casey liked hearing her dad refer to Brian as her "friend." At the same time, it made her uneasy. In a way, Brian *was* becoming her friend. The trouble was, she was afraid that was all he was becoming.

"Ten o'clock." She sighed, craning her neck to see the clock on the kitchen wall. It was only eight-thirty.

By the time Brian rang the doorbell, Casey was a nervous wreck. When she opened the door and saw Brian standing on the porch, she suddenly relaxed. Somehow, it seemed perfectly natural for him to be there.

"Hi," she said. "I see you brought your bike."

Brian smiled. "I thought we might want to take a test ride. To make sure we've got your gears right."

"It's really nice of you to do this," Casey said, opening the door wider. "Come in and meet my parents."

After she introduced Brian to her mom and dad, Casey led him out to the garage to show him her bike. He ran his fingers over the handlebars, then looked at the gear clusters and tried the brake levers. "Were you for real about it being a used bike?" he asked. "It looks like it's hardly been ridden."

"Maybe it does *now*," Casey said. "You should have seen it when I first got it. It was so messed up that I practically had to take the whole thing apart and put it back together again."

He glanced at the shelf where she had arranged her tools and spare parts. "I'm really impressed," he said.

"Thanks," Casey said. Maybe now she'd have one up on Leslie Duncan.

Brian was looking at the Challenger again. "Where did you learn about bikes?" he asked.

Casey pointed at the library books on the shelf next to the tools. "From those," she said. She picked up one of the books and opened the front cover. "I bet they're overdue. I forgot all about returning them. Maybe we could ride over to the library to test my gears."

"Sure," Brian said. "It's only a couple of miles." He stuck the books in his backpack and dropped the pack on the floor. He straightened up and turned back to the bike. "Let's take a look at that derailleur. Do you have a small screwdriver?"

Casey picked a screwdriver from the shelf and held it out to him. "What about this one?"

"Perfect," Brian said. He took the screwdriver and crouched beside the rear wheel of the bike. "That might do it," he said a few seconds later.

Casey stared at him. "Are you kidding? That's all there was to it? I've been trying to get it right for three days."

Brian looked at her with the same shy expression that he had worn when they talked about all the sports he played. "I've been working on bikes for a long time," he said. "You get a feel for it. But we won't know for sure that it's right until you try it."

They wheeled the bike outside. Casey threw her leg over the crossbar and put one foot on a pedal. All at once, Brian frowned. "Wait a minute," he said. "I think the bike's a little too big for you."

He lowered the seat and handlebars, then asked Casey to sit on the seat while he checked the fit. "The pedal reach is okay now," he said. "But you have to stretch to reach the brake levers."

Casey could see that he looked worried. "Is that bad?" she asked. After all the work she had done, she wasn't really sure she wanted to hear the answer.

"It could be a problem if you ever need to make a fast stop in a tight spot," Brian explained. "The trouble is, it's the frame that's too long, and there's no way to adjust that."

Casey's heart fell. She had spent three full weeks buying the bike and reconditioning it. Now, when she thought she finally had it made, there seemed to be more problems.

Brian must have seen the look of disappointment on her face, because he smiled and said, "Hey, I didn't mean to scare you. You can still ride it okay. Just pay attention to where you're going and be ready in case you have to go for the brakes fast."

Casey breathed a sigh of relief. "Okay. I'm going to try the gears now." She rode up the block and back, shifting through one gear after another. "It's much better," she said as she braked to a stop on the sidewalk. "But it's still a little hard to get into low gear. It might just be me," she added. "I haven't had much practice shifting."

Brian made another adjustment and said, "Try it again."

This time, Casey managed to shift smoothly through all the gears. "It's perfect," she said. "Now it's me I have to work on."

"You'll get used to it," Brian said. "Let me show you what I did, in case you need to adjust it again."

A few minutes later Casey told her mother they were going for a ride, and they set off for the library. Before she knew it, they were riding back up the street to her house. Then Brian was gone, and they *still* hadn't talked about anything but bikes.

But talking about bikes was *definitely* better than not talking at all, she decided. At least Brian had noticed her, and her bike was finally ready for the trip. All she had to do now was practice riding.

For a start, she decided to ride over to Laura's house. Laura was outside, watering the flowers near the front door. "Hi," she said. "How did it go?"

"Great," Casey said. "Everything works perfectly now."

Laura rolled her eyes in exasperation and put down the garden hose. "I meant, how did it go with Brian? You finally got to be alone with him, didn't you?"

"Yeah," Casey said. "Sure. He fixed my bike, then we rode over to the library to return the bike books."

Laura gave her a long look. "Then what?"

"Nothing," Casey said. "He went home, and I rode over to see you." The way Laura was looking at her made her uncomfortable. "Well, what did you expect?" she said defensively. "That's all he came over for."

"That's the problem," Laura said. "I thought he would at least ask you to go for a soda or something. Maybe you're going about this the wrong way."

Casey had been trying to hide her disappointment. Now Laura sounded so concerned that she couldn't keep her feelings in any longer. "I don't know," she said. "At first, I couldn't talk to him at all, and now all we can talk about is bikes. Sometimes I wonder if taking up biking has just made things worse."

Laura smiled sympathetically. "I feel so guilty," she said. "The whole thing was my idea to begin with. Are you sure you really want to go through with it?"

Once she had made up her mind to go on the trip, Casey had never even considered the possibility of backing out. But she had to admit that nothing had turned out quite as she had hoped. Maybe she *was* going about it the wrong way.

She thought about the Challenger and all the work she had put into it. Then she remembered dancing with Brian at the pool party. The way he had pulled her close had definitely felt special. The sound of his voice and the look in his eyes had been so romantic—until Leslie Duncan showed up.

"It's the only way I'll ever see him without Leslie," she said at last. "After all the work I've done, I'm not going to back out now."

"I know you've worked really hard for the trip," Laura said slowly. "But Leslie wasn't there when you saw him today, and nothing really happened."

"Yeah," Casey admitted. "But it was nice, anyway. I didn't say I expected him to fall madly in love with me, did I? All I wanted was to get to know him better. And, thanks to Leslie, I've barely got started. There's no way I'm going to give up now."

Laura grinned and shook her head. "You're unbelievable. Have you even let him know you're interested?" she asked. "I mean, Leslie certainly makes it clear to him that she likes him. You don't seem to give him any encouragement. Maybe he's waiting for you to make the first move."

"Maybe." Casey pondered her friend's comments for a moment, then said, "No, it's not me. Leslie's more brazen than I am. She doesn't mind chasing a boy. I can't do that."

"Well," Laura said, "I just hope you're not making a mistake."

All at once, Casey felt her confidence returning. Even though she had seen Brian often lately, until that morning, she had never been alone with him for more than a few minutes. Then she had felt more relaxed with him than ever. Brian had seemed more at ease, too. Spending four entire days together would give them plenty of time to think of something to talk about besides bikes. That day was just the beginning.

"I'm not making a mistake," she told Laura with a grin. "We just need more time together. Besides, I'm really starting to like biking."

Chapter Nine

Casey stood in front of the mirror fastening the strap of her safety helmet and wrinkling her nose in disgust. Since the past weekend when Brian had helped her adjust her gears, she had been riding her bike to work every day. But on Monday night her parents insisted that she buy the helmet and wear it whenever she rode on public streets. Now it was Thursday, and she still wasn't used to wearing the helmet. It made her head look like a bowling ball.

August was hot enough without having her head encased in a ball of black plastic. Besides, her parents would never know whether she wore it or not. Casey reached up to undo the strap, then she hesitated. Brian had told her that all serious bikers wore helmets, hadn't he?

Suddenly the bowling ball in the mirror looked

back at her in astonishment. It was incredible, but she was beginning to think of herself as a serious biker! She actually preferred riding her bicycle to riding in Laura's car. It felt as if she were soaring close to the ground, feeling the air and smelling the trees as she zipped through the streets.

Thinking about it reminded her of the dream she had had about riding with Brian. Maybe dreams could come true, she decided.

Still wearing the helmet, she went to the garage, wheeled her bike out, and locked the door behind her. A few minutes later she braked to a stop at Laura's front porch.

As soon as Laura opened the door, Casey could see that something was bothering her. "What's the matter?" she asked, immediately.

"I don't know," Laura said. "This whole summer has been just too weird."

Casey had an uneasy feeling that the weirdness had something to do with her. She walked into the living room and flopped down on the couch. "Do you think you could be a little more specific?"

Laura flopped down beside her and draped one leg over the arm of the couch. "Greg wants me to be his steady girlfriend," she said, sounding as though she were announcing a major airline disaster.

"What's so weird about that?" Casey asked cautiously.

"We've only been dating for a couple of weeks. Besides I hate being tied down."

"Then why don't you tell him you don't want to?"

Laura shrugged and twisted a loose thread in the hem of her shorts. "It's fun to have someone to hang out with," she said. "Especially now that you're so *busy* all the time. I practically need a bicycle if I want to talk to you."

Casey didn't even try to hide her astonishment. "The bike trip was *your* idea," she said.

"Sure," Laura said. "But I didn't expect you to make a career of it."

Suddenly Casey felt the same way she had felt when her parents lectured her about working too hard. Everyone wanted to tell her what to do, then as soon as she did it, they gave her a hard time.

"What makes you think Greg is going to drop you if you say no?" Casey asked, trying to move the conversation away from herself.

As soon as the words were out, Casey realized that wasn't really the problem. She had been afraid of losing Laura to Greg. Now Laura was afraid of losing Casey to bicycling, and she had been too preoccupied with her problems to realize it.

Laura had a right to be upset with her. They had been inseparable since they had first met. But ever since Casey had decided to go on the bike trip, they had been spending less and less time together.

Casey smiled guiltily. "I guess I haven't been a very good friend lately," she said. "I'm sorry."

Laura shrugged again and looked down at her hands. "You can't help it," she said. "You've been really busy."

"Maybe so," Casey said. "But that's no excuse. You're my best friend, and I want to keep it that way. Look, I don't have to work on my bike anymore. You and Greg just seemed so tight, I thought *you* were the one who was busy. Let's do something this Saturday night."

Laura looked sheepish. "I have a date with Greg on Saturday. I don't suppose you'd consider doubling with Ron Bradford."

Whenever Laura brought up doubling, Casey felt pressured. She didn't think she should have to date Ron in order to see Laura. That didn't make any more sense than saying Laura had to take up biking to be with her. "No," she said, at last. "Why don't we just go out for a soda or something Sunday afternoon?"

Laura's face brightened. "Okay," she agreed.

"Maybe afterward we can check out the new record store in the mall."

Seeing Laura's smile made Casey feel better. "Great," she said. "I wish I could stick around for a while, but I have to start work in twenty minutes. Let me know what you decide about going steady with Greg. Call me tonight if you want to talk about it." She waved to her friend and ran out to her bike.

Casey knew her job so well by then that she didn't have to think about it. If Brian didn't show up, being stuck in the snack stand could get very boring. He didn't come to the pool that day, but Casey tried to convince herself that it was just as well. At least she didn't have to watch Leslie Duncan hovering around him.

After work she took a long ride to help build her stamina for the trip. By the time she arrived at her house, it was almost six o'clock. Her parents were already in the kitchen fixing dinner.

"Brian Warner called," Mrs. Meadows said as soon as Casey walked in. "Isn't he the boy who came over to help with your bike?"

Casey nodded casually and pretended to adjust the strap on her safety helmet, but her heart was pounding like crazy. "What did he want?" she asked, trying to keep her voice normal.

"Something about a bike outing," her mother said. "He wants you to call him back."

When Casey heard that, she couldn't contain her excitement any longer. "Oh, wow!" she said. "Where's his number?"

Half a minute later she heard Brian's voice say "Hello" over the phone.

"Hi," she said. "This is Casey. My mom said you called."

"Yeah," Brian said. "I'm glad you called back. How's your bike?"

"Perfect," Casey said. "I've been riding it everywhere."

"Great. The reason I called is that some of the kids who are going on the trip are getting together for a training ride this Sunday. I thought you might like to go along."

Casey felt a confused mix of delight and disappointment. She was glad Brian had invited her, but she had been hoping he had something more personal in mind. "Sure," she said. "It sounds like fun, and I need all the practice I can get."

"Terrific," Brian said. "Everyone is meeting at the corner of Bradley and Hill streets. At two o'clock."

"I'll be there," Casey said.

"Okay," Brian said. "Talk to you later."

Casey felt a tiny thrill as she said "Good-bye" and put down the phone. Brian hadn't exactly asked her for a date, but at least he had thought of her. That was more than she could have said a few weeks before.

She went to the bathroom to wash up for dinner, then returned to the kitchen and started setting the table.

"Well?" Mrs. Meadows said.

"Well what?" Casey said as though her mom was making a big deal out of nothing. "Some kids are getting together for a training ride on Sunday. He invited me to go along."

She wondered if it was safe to tell her parents how she felt about Brian now. The trouble was, she was so used to being secretive that it was hard to talk about him. Besides, it wasn't as if he had really asked her for a date.

"He seems like a nice boy," Mrs. Meadows said.

"Yeah," Casey said. "I kind of like him." She opened a cupboard door to get the salt and pepper shakers, then suddenly she froze. "Oh, no! I forgot I'm supposed to go shopping with Laura on Sunday!"

"Don't look so tragic," Mrs. Meadows said.

"Surely, Laura will understand if you need to change your plans."

Casey grimaced. "Oh, no, she won't," she said. "She's already mad at me for not spending enough time with her."

After dinner Casey called Laura to tell her about the bike ride. "I'm really sorry," she said. "Maybe we could get together earlier in the day."

"It's okay," Laura said. "But I promised my folks I'd go with them to visit my grandmother on Sunday morning. We'll get together some other time."

As she hung up the phone, Casey thought that Laura had taken the news quite well. When Laura didn't call or come by for the next two days, though, she began to wonder. But by Saturday night, she was so excited about the bike ride that she forgot to worry about anything else.

Things were finally working out just as she had hoped. The next day she was going to spend the whole afternoon with Brian—and she *wouldn't* be stuck in the snack stand while Leslie worked on her diving with him. It was too good to be true, she thought as she drifted off to sleep.

She thought the same thing again when she

arrived at the corner of Bradley and Hill streets the next afternoon. It *was* too good to be true. A group of kids was waiting at the corner, but Brian was nowhere in sight.

Casey introduced herself, then listened while a girl in a dark green jogging suit pointed to a map and described the route. The girl was Sue Taylor. Apparently, she was in charge of the outing. "What we're going for is the uphills," she said. "Like the long, steep grades at Oak Creek."

Casey tried to pay attention, but all she could think about was Brian. She kept looking around, expecting to see him arrive. After a few minutes Sue threw her leg over her bike and led the way down Hill Street. The other bikers started to follow, and Casey reluctantly joined the pack.

When she thought about it, she remembered Brian hadn't actually said he was going to be there. She had just automatically assumed he would lead the outing. Now she could hardly conceal her disappointment. Like an idiot, she had looked forward to spending the afternoon with him. She had even broken her date with Laura, at the risk of making her friend more upset than ever.

But it was a good chance to meet some of the other kids who were going on the trip, and, with or without Brian, she needed the practice. After the first five miles or so, she was so caught up in the ride that she had almost forgotten about him. Then she looked up from shifting gears and saw him riding straight toward her. The next thing she knew, he was making a U-turn and falling in beside her, pedaling easily on his silver Eagle.

"Hi," he said. "How's it going?"

"Okay," Casey managed to say, breathless from pedaling uphill. Suddenly she couldn't think about anything but the sweat trickling down her neck and gluing her shirt to her back.

Someone had to make the first move, she decided, remembering Laura's words. Letting Brian know she was glad to see him didn't exactly mean she was chasing him. "I was afraid you weren't going to show up," she said.

Brian grinned at her, but his eyes looked serious. Casey felt another rush of excitement. "Sorry I was late," he said. "I guess you met the other kids."

Casey nodded, concentrating on trying to handle the bike and make conversation at the same time. There was a long hill ahead, and her excitement at having Brian there made her feel as though the temperature had risen ten degrees. Her legs were already tired, but she pedaled steadily because Brian was watching her. She didn't want him to think she wasn't up to the trip.

"You should get into low gear now," he said, all at once. Casey gave him a curious look. "Low-low?" she asked. She already knew that using her lowest gear on a flat surface made her feel as though she weren't pedaling at all. In high, she had to push harder on the pedals, but she got more speed and distance with each push.

"Whatever you need for the hill," Brian said, reaching for the shift lever on the Eagle. "Once you're into the upgrade, you can't pedal fast enough to make the shift."

Casey let out a loud groan and began to shift to low. "That's probably why my legs are so tired," she said. "I thought it was better to stay in high gear and try to get up some speed."

Brian looked sympathetic. "Everyone thinks that at first," he said. "But momentum won't take you very far on these grades. The pedaling gets rough if you're stuck in high."

The hill they were starting up was the steepest one yet. Even using her lowest gear, Casey felt as if she were ramming her feet into a brick wall every time she pushed the pedals. She glanced at Brian, saw him pedaling effortlessly beside her, and grinned awkwardly. She was embarrassed enough that she hadn't known when to shift her gears. Now, even though she had shifted correctly, she could barely make it up the hill. Brian probably wondered if she was even capable of going on the trip at all.

But she was keeping up with him, she realized after a minute. Or else he was staying back to ride with *her!* Either way she looked at it, Casey felt better. The pedaling got easier, and before she knew it, they had reached the top of the hill.

"Let's take it easy and rest on the downgrade," Brian said. "Don't worry about shifting up until you reach the flat." Casey nodded, then they were over the peak and soaring side-by-side down the hill. It was too good to be true, Casey thought again as she felt the breeze whipping past and cooling her bare arms. This was exactly what she had dreamed about.

When the street flattened out at the bottom of the hill, she heard Brian's gears shifting and reached for her own shift lever. Then she looked up and saw the Eagle pulling ahead of her. Brian looked back and waved. "Try to sit back farther in the seat," he called over his shoulder. "You'll get a better leg extension."

Before Casey had time to respond, Brian shot forward to overtake another rider. Casey's heart sank as she watched him fall in with a dark-haired boy she had met earlier. He had just been riding with her to help her get ready for the trip. Like a dope, she had imagined he was doing it because he liked her.

At last Brian Warner had noticed her, and now she was just another biker signed up for the Oak Creek Canyon trip. But at least they were spending time together, Casey reminded herself. And she still had the trip to look forward to.

Chapter Ten

For the first time in weeks, Casey woke up without feeling that she had to jump instantly out of bed to do something. It was Thursday, and the trip was exactly one week away. Her bike was perfect now, and her confidence about riding in Oak Creek Canyon had grown steadily since the training ride the past Sunday.

The only thing that was really bothering her now was Laura. Whenever she called her, Laura always said she was busy, but Casey never quite believed her. She was sure Laura was still mad at her for canceling their shopping trip.

Casey was unhappy with the situation, but as long as Laura refused to talk about it, there was no way she could make it right. In the meantime, Casey had to worry about where she was going to get a sleeping bag. She had planned on borrowing Laura's, but now that Laura was mad at her, that idea was out of the question.

She couldn't afford to buy one of her own, either. Casey still had to get a backpack, give her dad another fifty dollars for the bike, and pay the balance on the trip fee. The next day was payday, but her check would only go so far. Casey sighed and sat up in bed. Every time she thought she was going to get a chance to sleep in, she woke up thinking about some new problem. Her parents were probably as tired of hearing about money as she was, but she had to talk to them about it again.

She hauled herself out of bed and stumbled down the hall to the kitchen, still wearing her pajamas. " 'Morning," she said, putting her hand over her mouth to cover a yawn.

"Good morning," her mother said. "I thought maybe you were going to sleep in for a change."

"I was," Casey said. "But I needed to talk to you."

Her father smiled and put down the newspaper. "It must be important to get you out of bed while you're still half-asleep."

Casey nodded, then propped her elbow on the table and cupped her chin in her hand. "It is," she said. "I know you must be tired of hearing about this, but I'm afraid I'm not going to have enough money to pay for everything before the trip."

"That does sound serious," Mr. Meadows said.

"Would it help if we gave you more time to pay back the loan on your bike?" Mrs. Meadows asked after a moment.

Casey's eyes came wide open. "Would it *help*?" she exclaimed. "It would practically solve all my problems!"

"Good," Mr. Meadows said. "But this doesn't mean you can just forget the debt. If you can't pay for it out of your earnings, we'll work out a plan to deduct it from your allowance."

"Fine," said Casey. "You can even charge me interest."

"I don't think that's necessary," Mrs. Meadows said. "But it's responsible of you to offer."

"Thanks," Casey said. "I think I'll go back to bed now."

But as she sank back into bed, she couldn't help wondering if her parents had made her pay for the trip just to teach her to be more responsible. If they had, maybe it was working. She didn't really mind her job at the pool, and Brian seemed impressed that she had reconditioned her own bike. When she thought about it, she was impressed, too.

It was incredible how Brian had changed her life, without even knowing it. One more week, and they would be biking together in Oak Creek Canyon. If only Laura weren't mad at her, life would be perfect.

When Casey got off work that afternoon, she thought about riding over to Laura's house and trying to work things out. She couldn't think of anything new to say since the last time she had tried, so she decided to ride up Hill Street, instead.

Sitting farther back on the seat, as Brian suggested, made it harder to reach the brakes, but it also made it easier to pedal. Between that and knowing when to shift, she could ride for miles without getting tired. Finally, she decided she had better start home if she didn't want to be late for dinner.

Approaching an intersection and the last up-grade on the way home, she started shifting into low. Just as she started into the intersection, she heard a car coming up behind her. Suddenly it was beside her, then she realized it was starting to make a right turn directly across her path.

After that, everything seemed to happen in slow motion. The car was practically in front of her, and the driver didn't even know she was there! In another second she was going to run straight into it. Frantically, she jerked the handlebars to the right and grabbed for the brakes.

The car sped past just as she felt the front wheel of the bike collide with the curb. The next thing she knew, she was sprawled on the sidewalk with her bicycle on top of her.

For a moment she was too stunned to move. The driver who ran her off the road hadn't even stopped!

Casey got up, slightly dazed. The Challenger seemed to have come through without a scratch, but she wasn't so lucky. When she stood up, her left ankle started to throb painfully.

She thought about calling her parents to pick her up but immediately decided against it. Her ankle was probably just twisted. It was already beginning to feel better. If her parents found out about it, they might not let her go on the trip.

Nothing was going to stop her from going on the trip, she told herself determinedly. By doing most of the pedaling with her right foot, she managed to ride the rest of the way home. The ankle still hurt when she parked the bike in the garage. She forced herself to walk normally, and her parents didn't seem to notice anything.

But when she woke up the next morning, she wasn't sure she could walk without limping, let alone ride her bike. Her ankle was so sore and swollen that she stayed in bed so that her parents wouldn't see it.

The next time she woke up, it was after ten o'clock. She couldn't afford to miss a day at work, and she had less than two hours to get there. Somebody had to give her a ride.

Normally, Casey wouldn't have hesitated to ask Laura, but now she was reluctant. They hadn't spoken at all in days. Finally she decided she didn't have any choice. Even though Laura was mad at her, she would have to call her and ask her for help.

She sat up, then hobbled to the phone and dialed Laura's number.

"Hi," she said. "I know you're mad at me, but you've *got* to help me."

"What's wrong now?" Laura asked. She managed to make it sound as though Casey was nothing but trouble. After Casey told her about the accident, she started to sound friendlier. "You're crazy not to tell your parents," she said. "It could be broken or something."

"It'll be okay in a couple of days," Casey said. "Besides, if I tell my folks, they probably won't let me go on the trip."

"Okay," Laura said, at last. "I'll drive you to work. But if you end up in the hospital, I'm not responsible."

Even though Laura was trying to act indifferent, her voice sounded concerned. Casey felt a rush of gratitude. "Sure," she said. "It's really great of you to help me out. I hope this means we can be friends again."

Laura was silent for a moment. "I guess," she said, at last. "It's just been a weird summer."

"I know," Casey said. "But just because things are changing, it doesn't mean we have to stop being friends. I don't know what I would do around here without you."

"Me, either," Laura said. "I'm sorry I've been acting like such a dope. Why don't I come over early and bring my sleeping bag?"

Half an hour later Laura arrived and handed Casey the sleeping bag. "Thanks," Casey said. "I was wondering where I was going to get one. I couldn't ask for yours while you were mad at me."

Laura gave an embarrassed grin. "I know," she said. "I was worrying about it, too."

Casey grinned back and went to get some sodas from the refrigerator. After that, they sat around talking as though nothing had been wrong between them.

At five minutes to twelve, Laura dropped Casey off at the pool. Casey limped slowly toward the snack stand. As long as she didn't put too much weight on her left foot, she could get around. If she forgot for a second and walked normally, a dull pain shot through her ankle.

She was so busy concentrating on walking carefully that she didn't see Brian until he was almost standing in front of her. "Hi," he said. "What happened to your foot?"

Casey told him about the accident. As he listened, his green eyes glinted with anger. "Some drivers don't even see bicycles," he said. "They run you off the road and don't even know it happened."

Casey had never seen him angry before. "It could have been worse," he explained. "You were lucky you could get out of the way."

Seeing how upset he was, Casey wondered if it was because he was worried about her, personally. He was probably just fed up with careless drivers, in general, she decided. It sounded as if he had trouble with them, too.

"Anyway," she said, "I just twisted my ankle when I fell. It's not a big deal."

"Let's see," Brian said, squatting down to look at the ankle. He touched it so gently that Casey hardly felt it. "It's kind of swollen," he said. "Have you been to a doctor?"

Casey shook her head, feeling like a dope. There was no way she could tell him she intended to go on the trip even if she had two broken legs and an appendicitis attack before next Thursday. "I don't want to worry my folks," she said casually. "I'm afraid they'll make a big thing about biking."

Brian gave her a long look, but he seemed to

understand. "It's probably just a slight sprain," he said. "But you should get it checked out."

He stood up, and Casey shrugged and managed an embarrassed smile. From the way Brian's expression changed, she could see that he didn't think the injury was serious. She was surprised at how relieved she felt. Maybe it was because Brian was a senior counselor on the trip. She had been worrying about her parents saying she couldn't go. Until now it hadn't occurred to her that Brian might do the same thing.

"If it doesn't get better in a couple of days, I'll go to the doctor," she said.

Of course, she knew it was going to get better. It *had* to! It was astonishing how much she was looking forward to the trip—even aside from being with Brian. After everything she had done that summer, she felt incredibly independent. She would be going on vacation *without* her parents. And, she could hardly wait to see how the bike performed on the long hills through Oak Creek Canyon.

Chapter Eleven

At last it was time to leave! Casey had finished her last day at work the day before, and her ankle was so much better that she had almost forgotten about it. She hadn't ridden her bike since the accident, although she had been swimming to keep in shape. Laura had been driving her to work and back, and they had been spending most of their free time together.

Life couldn't be more perfect, Casey thought. She and Laura were friends again, and in a few hours she would be on her way to Oak Creek Canyon with Brian.

She hefted her outdoor bag onto her bed and checked it again to make sure she had packed everything she needed. She considered packing her blow dryer, then decided there probably wouldn't be any electricity where she was going.

It was ridiculous, the way she was fussing about everything. But she had worked hard for this trip, and she wanted it to be perfect.

She zipped the outdoor bag, carried it into the living room, and put it down beside her backpack and sleeping bag. The kids going on the trip were meeting in the school yard at noon. Mr. Meadows was taking an early lunch so he could drive Casey over with her bike and gear. Casey checked her gear again and decided there was nothing left to do until her dad came to pick her up.

Around ten-thirty the phone rang. Casey ran to answer it, thinking it would be Laura calling to say "goodbye" again. When she heard Brian's voice instead, she nearly flipped.

"I thought I'd come by in the van and pick you up," he said. "If you don't have a bike rack for your car, it might be hard to get your bike and gear there in one trip."

Casey couldn't believe this was happening. "That would be really nice," she said. Her bicycle would easily fit into the trunk of her dad's car, but this was an opportunity she couldn't pass up!

"Okay!" Brian said. "Around eleven-thirty?"

"I'll be ready," Casey said.

As soon as she hung up the phone, Casey picked it up again to call her dad. "You won't have to leave work early," she said. "Brian Warner just called and offered to pick me up."

"Brian Warner," her dad said. "The same Brian Warner that you 'kind of like'?" From the sound of his voice, Casey could tell that he was teasing her. She had been trying to keep her feelings about Brian secret until she found out how he felt about her. Now she suspected that her parents had already guessed how much she liked him.

"Yeah," she said. "You knew all along, didn't you?"

"Knew what?" Mr. Meadows said, pretending to sound innocent.

Casey giggled. "You know. That I liked Brian."

"Your mother and I had our suspicions," he said. "Brian seems to be a nice boy. I hope everything will work out."

"Me, too," Casey said. "I'll tell you all about it when I get back."

"Okay. Take care, sweetheart. And have fun."

"Thanks, Dad. I will. Say 'bye to Mom again for me."

Things were getting off to a great start, Casey decided as she hung up the phone. Maybe Brian was looking forward to being with *him*. Why else would he have offered to pick her up?

Unless the counselors were picking up everyone. Casey's spirits sank—until Brian arrived alone!

"I'm glad you're one of the trip counselors," she told him. "It'll be a lot more fun with you there." It wasn't exactly a declaration of love, but at least she had told him she liked his company.

Brian turned away abruptly and lifted her bike into the van.

"I'm glad you decided to come on the trip, too," he said. "I've been looking forward to it. I've never been to Oak Creek Canyon."

"You're kidding," Casey said. "I thought everyone had been there but me."

"That makes two of us, then." Brian smiled and then added, "I think that's everything. We've got your bike, helmet, pack, water bottle, and clothes. Did you bring an extra pair of shoes? It helps to change if your feet get tired."

Casey nodded and pointed down at her high-tops. "These and my sneakers."

"Good," Brian said. "We're ready to go."

"It's really nice of you to do this," Casey said again, as he opened the door of the van for her.

Brian shrugged. "It's nothing," he said. "It's part of my job to make sure your bike and gear are in order."

Casey swallowed hard to keep from groaning. Here she was having fantasies about being with

Brian on the trip, and Brian only thought of her as just another biker.

On the way over to Northside High, Brian told her more about the trip. Twelve kids were going, plus Ms. Williams and Mr. Ramsey, the chaperons. Six kids were assigned to each van. Once they got to the campground, they would stake out separate areas for boys and girls and pitch tents. The bike rides would follow different routes each day, and the vans would go along to provide lunches and pick up stragglers, if necessary.

When Brian drove the van into the school yard, Ms. Williams was already calling out the names of the kids riding in her van. Casey heard her name called and went to shift her bike to the other van. "I guess I'll see you when we get there," Brian said, reaching to help her with the bike. "I'm assigned to Mr. Ramsey."

"Okay," Casey said, smiling too brightly in an effort to hide her disappointment. "See you later."

After she finished stowing her gear, she climbed into Ms. Williams's van and sat down beside the dark-haired boy she had met on the training ride. She watched Brian load his van, climb in, and check to see that the back doors were secured. As he turned around to look for a seat, she saw a tall, blond-haired girl stand up and wave at him.

Casey's mouth fell open in shock. The girl was Leslie Duncan! It was impossible, Casey told herself. She had spent half the summer working for this trip just so she could be with Brian without Leslie's interruptions. Leslie had never said a word about going on the trip, too. Now there she was in Brian's van!

It wasn't fair! Just when everything was going well, Leslie had to show up again.

All at once Casey understood what people meant when they talked about "seeing red." She was so furious that she felt as if her face were on fire. She wanted to leap out of the van, dash over to Leslie, and give her a piece of her mind.

She forced herself to calm down and glanced at the boy sitting next to her. She saw him looking at her and ordered herself to act human. "Hi," she said. The boy smiled.

"Hi, I'm Tim. Your name's Casey, isn't it? We met on the training ride."

After that, Casey tried to forget about Leslie and enjoy herself. Tim was friendly and talkative. Soon, he had everyone laughing and telling bike stories. Casey tried to join in, but her heart wasn't in it. Forgetting about Leslie Duncan was the same as trying not to scratch a mosquito bite.

When they arrived at the campsite several hours later, Casey was still irritated. But as soon as she stepped out of the van, her excitement returned. The canyon, full of strangely shaped rock formations and forests of oak trees, was as beautiful as everyone had said. A light breeze stirred the leaves and made the air feel soft and cool.

There was something incredibly romantic about Oak Creek Canyon, Casey decided immediately. It was so remote and quiet that she felt as though she had been transported to an enchanted world. Then she saw Leslie walking toward her. Why did fairy tales always have to include witches and ogres?

"Hi," she said before Leslie had a chance to say it first. Suddenly she was no longer intimidated by the pretty head cheerleader. "I didn't know you were planning to come on the trip."

Leslie's smile was instant and perfect, as usual. "I decided at the last minute," she said. "The way you and Brian kept talking about it, I was afraid I'd be missing out on something great."

"I'm sure," Casey said.

Either Leslie didn't get the message, or she was determined to ignore it. "It's really beautiful here," she said. "It's going to be fun, don't you think?"

What Casey really thought was that if she had the power to make Leslie vanish, she wouldn't hesitate for a split second. Fortunately, at just that moment Ms. Williams blew a whistle and called all the girls together.

"We'll pitch two tents over there," she said, pointing to the left side of the campground. "The boys will be on the opposite side. Toilet facilities are in that building in between. Girls on the left, boys on the right."

While Casey helped set up the camp, she prayed that she wouldn't get stuck with Leslie as a tent mate. Seeing Leslie hover at Brian's side was bad enough without having to listen to her talk about him every night while she was trying to get to sleep.

She breathed a sigh of relief when she learned that she was sharing a tent with Sue Taylor and a girl named Amy. Casey already knew Sue, the second senior counselor on the trip, from the training ride. Amy was a short, chunky, athletic-looking girl with a pleasant face.

"I've never slept in a tent," Amy said as the girls set up their cots and arranged their gear. "It feels like a cave."

Casey stared at the domed ceiling of the small

tent and grinned. "I see what you mean. I don't think we'll be spending a lot of time in here."

"Don't tell me I'm with a couple of claustrophobics," Sue said, teasing them. She flopped down on her sleeping bag and started telling a funny story about her claustrophobic uncle getting trapped in a telephone booth. By the time the story ended, they were all laughing as though they were old friends.

Suddenly Sue glanced at her watch and leapt to her feet. "I almost forgot. I'm supposed to be helping get things ready for the cookout."

"It's about time," Casey said. "I'm starving."

"Then you're recruited for kitchen duty," Sue said. "Get your tail in gear."

Casey wrinkled her nose in distaste, but actually she was relieved. She had been dying to see Brian. At the same time, though, she'd been dreading going out and finding him in Leslie's clutches. Maybe helping with the cookout would keep her too busy to notice.

As it turned out, she found herself standing beside Brian, setting out paper cups and hamburger buns. "How's it going?" Brian asked. "Did you get settled?"

"Everything's going just fine," Casey told him. "I really like my tent mates, and I can't believe this scenery."

"I guess you didn't get stuck with Ms. Williams," he said.

"Huh-uh." Or Leslie Duncan, either, Casey added silently. "I'm with Sue and Amy," she said aloud. "They're fun. What's the matter with Ms. Williams?"

Brian thought about it for a minute. "Actually, there's nothing wrong with her. She's pretty easygoing, for a chaperon. It's just that it's more fun to be with kids your own age."

"For sure," Casey said. "What about you?"

Brian grinned. "I'm with two of the guys. Would you hand me that jar of mustard?"

As Casey handed him the mustard, she was amazed at how comfortable she finally felt with Brian. She wondered if he felt the same way.

"I guess that's it," Brian said. "Let's go get a hamburger." He handed Casey a paper plate, and they walked over to the grill where Mr. Ramsey was cooking.

After they got their hamburgers, Casey looked around at the other kids, wondering where to sit. "There are seats over there," Brian said, pointing to a bench off by itself under a huge pine tree. "I've had enough of crowds for one day."

Casey's heart skipped a beat. At last they were going to be alone together. She walked over and sat down, determined to talk about something other than bikes, for a change.

"I can't believe this summer," she said. "So much has happened."

Brian swallowed a bite of hamburger and turned to face her. "Biking, you mean?"

"Not just that," Casey said. "'Getting a job, and reconditioning the bike, and having my best friend mad at me because I was so busy." She suddenly stopped talking and glanced down at her plate. "I guess it sounds dumb, but I've always been more easygoing than ambitious. I usually spend my summers lying around in the sun."

"I wish I could say that about myself," Brian said. "I'm not particularly ambitious, but I wouldn't say I'm easygoing, either. I always take on about twice as much as I can actually do."

"You must really love sports," Casey said.

Brian's mouth lifted in a crooked smile. "Not as much as you might think," he said. "It's just that most sports seem to come naturally to me. Sometimes I feel that if I say no to coaching a baseball team or something, I'm wasting a gift." He reached for his hamburger. "You probably think *that* sounds dumb."

Casey smiled and shook her head. It didn't sound dumb, but it made her wonder if that was why Brian had helped her so much with biking. It would have been nicer to think he had done it because he liked her.

She was trying to think of a way to tell him that, when she heard a twig snap behind her. The next thing she knew, Leslie Duncan was standing next to their bench.

"Hi, Brian. Hi, Casey. It's a terrific night, isn't it? I love being out here in the woods."

Leslie always managed to show up at the absolute worse moment! Whatever Casey had wanted to say to Brian would now have to wait.

Casey realized that Leslie could turn her dream trip into a terrible nightmare. The problem was that once Leslie turned up she was there to stay. Keeping Leslie Duncan away from her and Brian would clearly be Casey's greatest accomplishment of the summer.

Chapter Twelve

"Breakfast in half an hour," Sue called.

Casey blinked and stared up at the top of the tent for a second. Then she remembered where she was and scrambled out of her cot.

A few minutes later she stood in the washroom waiting for her turn in the shower. Ms. Williams had said there was only one shower for all six of them, but Casey hadn't figured everyone would show up at the same time.

"She's been in there forever," Amy complained. "At this rate, we'll never get breakfast."

"Yeah," Sue called, using her authority as senior counselor. "Give somebody else a chance."

When the shower door finally opened, Leslie Duncan emerged with a thick, blue towel wrapped around her head. "Sorry," she said. "I thought everyone else was up hours ago."

135

"Sure," Amy said as she pumped a handful of quarters into the hot-water meter. "I *always* try to shower before daylight."

Amy stomped into the shower, and Casey watched out of the corner of her eye while Leslie carefully inspected herself in the mirror. How could anyone look so good so early in the morning? Casey wondered.

Casey's mind went back to the evening before. She had probably been dumb to walk away when Leslie butted in on her and Brian, but Leslie was so overwhelming when she was in action. Casey wondered how Brian felt about her.

Suddenly she was eager to see Brian and decided to take her shower later. She washed up at the sink next to Leslie, then returned her gear to the tent and went to get breakfast.

Unfortunately, Brian was not among the group of kids surrounding Mr. Ramsey at the cooking fire. Casey smelled bacon frying and realized she was starving. At least the food line was moving faster than the shower line.

Casey was just finishing up her last bite of eggs when Ms. Williams blew her whistle and called the group to attention. "We'll be setting out in about half an hour," she said. "The vans will go on ahead to set up lunch camp."

Sue and Brian stepped forward where everyone could see them. "You all know our senior counselors by now," Ms. Williams went on. "They'll be checking up on you along the road. You're going to be spreading out, but try to keep one another in sight. If you get separated, don't worry. Just keep riding and wait for Sue or Brian to find you."

Until now, Casey had been so preoccupied with Brian and Leslie that she had almost forgotten why she was there. But with the day's ride about to start, she felt a rush of excitement. Glancing over at her bike, she couldn't resist smiling when she saw its red paint gleaming in the morning sunlight.

"Time to put it to the test," she heard someone say. She turned around and found Brian smiling back at her.

"Hi," she said. "I'm a little nervous."

"There's nothing to worry about," Brian said. "Especially not with that bike," he added. "How's your ankle?"

Casey stared at him blankly for a second before she realized what he was talking about. "It's fine," she said quickly. "I totally forgot about it."

"It might start acting up again when you put a strain on it," Brian said. "I could put an elastic bandage around it, if you want."

Casey hesitated. She was certain she didn't need to bandage her ankle, and the last thing she wanted was to draw attention to it. Then she saw Leslie Duncan watching them and changed her mind. "If you think my ankle needs it, sure," she replied.

She sat down on a bench and waited until Brian went to get the bandage. When he returned, Leslie was still watching. Casey was sure Leslie must be jealous of the attention Brian was giving her. "It's really nice of you to do this," she said, glancing at Leslie and smiling, rubbing it in some more.

"That's why I'm here," Brian said lightly. He began winding the bandage around her foot and ankle.

All at once, Casey wished she hadn't chosen just that moment to try to teach Leslie a lesson. Why did Brian have to remind her that she was just another biker every time she started to think he liked her?

The next thing she knew, Leslie was standing right beside her. She was wearing powder blue shorts and a tank top, and her hair gleamed in the sunlight as though it were gold. Her sneakers were the same color as the rest of her outfit, and Casey wondered if she had a powder blue safety helmet, as well.

"What's wrong with your ankle?" Leslie said.

"Nothing," Casey said. "I twisted it awhile ago, but it's okay now."

Leslie cocked her head to one side and looked skeptical. "Then why is Brian bandaging it?"

"Just to make sure," Brian said. "Wiggle your foot, Casey."

"I hope it isn't serious," Leslie said. "It's such a great day. It would be awful if you couldn't ride."

Casey wanted to scream. She knew Leslie must be making a fuss just to impress Brian, and she'd had about all she could take.

"I'm *sure*," she answered, not bothering to hide her sarcasm.

Leslie's eyebrows shot up. "Well, excuse me," she said. "I can see when I'm not welcome." She turned abruptly and walked away.

Casey breathed a sigh of relief. Then she looked at Brian. She couldn't read his expression, but something about it made her wish she had kept her mouth shut.

There was no time to worry, though. The other kids were gathering behind Sue with their bikes. Casey rushed to get her bicycle and joined them. A few seconds later they set off down the highway with Sue in the lead.

Biking was better than she had ever imagined, Casey decided awhile later. The streets where she'd ridden at home seemed to be city sidewalks compared to the long, graceful slopes through Oak Creek Canyon. She was so close to the trees that she almost felt as if she were riding through the forest itself.

She shifted smoothly into low gear for an upcoming hill, then tilted her head back to feel the sun and breeze on her face. Amy, riding just ahead of her, looked back over her shoulder and grinned. Casey waved, then glanced around at the other bikers.

They had all started out in a clump, but now they were beginning to spread out along the highway. She could just see Leslie Duncan a half mile or so ahead of her, taking the lead. Tim was still right behind Casey, and they called out to one another as they pedaled single file up the steep grade.

Halfway up, Casey noticed a dull ache in her left ankle and began to slow down. Tim crept past her, then waved as he pulled ahead. By the time she reached the crest of the hill, he had disappeared from sight.

Casey pedaled slowly, trying to do most of the work with her right foot. After a while she glanced over her shoulder and saw that there was nobody behind her. The silence was spooky.

The dappled shadows of the trees danced eerily on the pavement, and the breeze sent a chill down her spine.

She heard a car approaching behind her and tightened her grip on the handlebars. There was plenty of room for bikes on the wide shoulder of the highway, but knowing that didn't help. The crunch of tires against the pavement reminded her of the car that had run her off the road, and her knees went weak with panic. Then the car whizzed by, and the silence returned.

Casey had never felt so alone in her life. The night before she had imagined she was in an enchanted world. Now the magic forest had turned into a dark maze filled with strange rustlings and ghostly shadows.

Recalling Ms. Williams's briefing before they set out, she forced herself to pedal steadily and watch the road ahead. Then she saw a flash of silver far in the distance. It had to be Brian coming back to check on her.

He was so far away that he seemed to be a speck on the horizon. Casey had never been so glad to see anyone in her entire life. Then she remembered Brian's expression during her conversation with Leslie.

The way Brian had stared at her was irritating—

as if *she* were the one who was out of line. But, then, what did he care if Leslie ruined her whole summer? He was just doing his job. She had been foolish to imagine there was anything else to it.

The whole thing was too embarrassing. By the time Brian reached her, Casey almost wished he hadn't come. "Hi," she said, determined not to make a fool of herself again. "It's a fabulous day, isn't it?"

Brian smiled and nodded, but his green eyes seemed to look right through her. "Are you okay?" he asked. "How's the ankle?"

Casey avoided his eyes. "It's fine," she said. "I just felt like taking my time." Aware that he was watching her, she forced herself to smile and push the pedals with both feet.

"I thought you might be getting tired," Brian said after a minute. "We could stop and rest for a while, if you want."

A few hours before Casey would have jumped at such a chance; now it was the last thing she wanted. With Leslie riding so far ahead of her, Casey knew she had to keep going to look good. "I don't want to rest," she said. "How much farther is it to lunch camp?"

"About three miles," Brian said. "Some of the kids are already there."

Casey ordered herself to keep smiling. "I'm starving," she said. "I'll be there soon."

Brian looked at her curiously, then rode off. He turned around once and waved. As Casey watched him disappear, she wanted to cry. She had spent half the summer trying to get to know Brian, and now he probably thought she was stubborn on top of being nasty to Leslie.

By the time she rode into lunch camp, the other kids had almost finished eating. Brian came to meet her and handed her a sandwich and a small bottle of juice. "Ms. Williams wants to look at your ankle," he said. His voice seemed cold, and when Casey looked at him, he avoided her eyes.

How could he? Casey thought furiously. He had told on her to Ms. Williams. "Why?" she asked. "I *told* you my ankle was okay."

Brian shrugged and looked guilty. Casey glared back at him for a second, then turned and walked away.

"It's not swollen," Ms. Williams said a few minutes later. "If it still looks okay in the morning, you can ride again tomorrow."

Casey was incredulous. "You mean I can't finish the ride *today*?"

"I'm afraid not," Ms. Williams said. "After lunch I'll be driving back to camp. You can ride in the van with me."

"That's not fair," Casey said. "I don't see why I have to be stuck in the van, just because Brian Warner thinks I can't ride."

"I'm sorry, Casey," she heard Brian say. "But if you ride this afternoon and keep straining that ankle, you probably won't be able to ride for the rest of the trip."

At the sound of his voice, Casey whirled around and glared at him. "You're not responsible for me," she said coolly.

Ms. Williams answered, "But the school *is* responsible for you."

Brian looked down and traced a line in the dirt with the toe of one shoe. Finally he looked up and shrugged. "You don't have any choice," he said. "It's either that or go home."

Casey was speechless. Nothing was turning out the way she had imagined it. Now, after being stuck in the snack stand all summer, she was going to be stuck in the van while Leslie rode with Brian. "I *might as well* go home," she said. Fighting back the tears, she went out to get her bike.

"Let me help you with it," Brian said as she started to lift it into the van. Casey tugged it out of his grip. "It's all right," she said. "I can do it myself." They stared at each other for a second, then Brian turned on his heel and walked away.

Two hours later Casey sat on a bench, fluffing her hair with her fingers while it dried in the sun. In a way, she was relieved to be back in camp taking it easy. At least, she hadn't had to wait in line to take a shower. And even though her ankle didn't really hurt, it was definitely tired.

What *did* really hurt was the way Brian had been acting. Giving her that strange look when she was sarcastic to Leslie was bad enough. Then he had to tell Ms. Williams about her ankle! It was enough to make her wonder if he was the nice guy she had thought he was, after all.

By the time the other kids arrived back at the campground, it was almost four-thirty. Casey went out of her way to avoid Brian, but she didn't have to work very hard at it. He seemed to be avoiding her, too. Then, while they were all sitting around the campfire after dinner, he came over and sat down beside her.

"I'm really sorry about what happened," he said. "But Ms. Williams was right; your ankle was too weak. I guess I was dumb to let you make the trip to begin with."

"Brian, you don't have to look out for me," Casey retorted. Immediately she wished she hadn't said it. She was angry, but he was still Brian. She had worked so hard all summer just to get to know him. Now that she finally had some time with him, it was foolish for her to be so rude. Besides, *she* was the one who was dumb for coming on the trip. It wasn't Brian's fault that she couldn't compete with Leslie Duncan.

Before she could think of anything else to say, Leslie walked up to them. "It's too bad you couldn't finish the ride today," she said to Casey. "I hope your ankle will be better tomorrow."

Just looking at Leslie made Casey furious again. "There's nothing wrong with my ankle," she said, determined not to lose her temper again. Why couldn't Leslie just go away and leave her alone?

Brian looked as though he wanted to say something and then changed his mind. Instead, he shook his head, stood up and turned away, with Leslie tagging along at his side. Watching them walk away, Casey had an empty feeling inside.

The whole trip had turned into a disaster. For a moment Casey wondered if she really should just go home and forget about Brian. So far, the trip certainly hadn't brought them any closer. But the more she thought about Leslie,

the more angry she became. There was probably nothing Leslie would like better than to get
rid of her.

With that realization, Casey was more determined than ever to stick it out and have a good
time. She had spent her whole summer working for this trip, and she wasn't going to let
Leslie Duncan ruin it for her. If it was competition Leslie wanted, it was competition she was
going to get!

Chapter Thirteen

Casey barely had time to open her eyes the next morning before Amy came stomping into the tent and flopped down on her sleeping bag. "If you were planning to shower, forget it," Amy said. "Leslie has taken over the washroom again."

Casey was struggling to get out of her sleeping bag, but her eyes weren't awake enough to focus on the zipper. "She's probably just used to having her own bathroom," she mumbled.

"Sure," Sue chimed in. "I suppose that's why she has to show off all the time with her bike. I practically wore my legs off yesterday trying to keep up with her. She kept taking the lead, even though she knew she was supposed to be following me."

Casey blinked and sat up straight, still trapped in the sleeping bag. As incredible as it seemed,

148

she was starting to feel sorry for Leslie Duncan. Leslie was supposed to be one of the most popular girls in school, but it seemed as though nobody actually liked her.

Nobody except Brian Warner. Considering the circumstances, Casey decided, it was ridiculous to start feeling sorry for Leslie. "Somebody get me out of this thing," she said. "Then let's just wash up and go get breakfast. I still have to let Ms. Williams check my ankle before the ride."

"I hope it'll be okay today," said Sue. "It would be a drag to have to hang around camp all day."

"I *know* it'll be okay," Casey said. "But hanging around camp wouldn't be so bad. At least I'd get to take a shower."

Sue and Amy both laughed. But only a few months before, Casey realized she would have really wanted to stay at the campsite relaxing all day. She had always been easygoing until the bike trip. Now she was spending every minute of her life either struggling to accomplish something or competing with Leslie Duncan. Sometimes, she hardly recognized herself.

A short time later Ms. Williams said she could ride again, and Casey was relieved. Instead of trying so hard to keep up, though, Casey decided she would relax and take it easy. There was no point in straining her ankle again, and she might not get another chance to enjoy the Oak Creek Canyon scenery for a long time.

Surprisingly, some of the other kids seemed to feel the same way. Either that, or they were just being nice. For the first few miles, Amy rode alongside her. "I'm glad I got you and Sue for my tent mates," Amy said.

"Me, too," Casey said, grinning as she recalled how she had dreaded getting stuck with Leslie. "I wish we could stay here longer. It's so beautiful, and riding here is so peaceful. I can't believe school starts next week."

After a while Amy decided to speed up, and Tim reappeared out of nowhere. "I think you've got the right idea by not rushing," he said. "This is a lot harder than I expected."

By midmorning, though, even Tim and Amy had gone on ahead, and Casey found herself alone again. It was crazy, the way she had felt so panicky the day before. Now that she had made up her mind to take it easy, Oak Creek Canyon seemed incredibly peaceful.

Then she saw Brian riding toward her on his silver bike, and her calm mood ended. She was still mad at him for telling Ms. Williams about her ankle, and she was annoyed that he seemed to enjoy Leslie's constant flirting. He obviously hadn't done anything to discourage it. But then, that wasn't so surprising, considering Leslie was one of the most gorgeous, not to mention athletic, girls at Northside High.

Just thinking about it was depressing. Competing with Leslie was impossible. If Brian thought Leslie was so terrific, Casey decided as Brian rode up to her and made a U-turn, then maybe she should just give up. But one sidelong look at him and Casey knew she was not ready to give up yet.

"Hi," she said. "How's it going?"

Brian's smile looked shy. "It's easier today. Everyone's slowing down a little."

It had never occurred to Casey that being a counselor could be hard work. She remembered Brian telling her how he felt that his athletic ability was almost a responsibility and wondered if he really just wanted to be a regular biker on the trip.

"You make looking out for a bunch of us seem so easy," she said. "You and Sue must be totally exhausted."

"Not totally," Brian said, then suddenly he hit his brakes and pointed off to the side of the road. "Look over there!"

Casey skidded to a stop and saw a doe and two tiny, spotted fawns watching them from the edge of the woods. She looked at Brian and smiled. "They're so cute, the way they're just standing there watching us watch them," she whispered.

"It makes you think, doesn't it?" Brian whispered back. "I mean, I wonder what they think of us."

"Do you really think they think?" Casey asked. It sounded so ridiculous that she and Brian both laughed at the same moment.

"I don't know," he said. "Well"— he smiled at her—"if you're okay, I guess I'd better get going."

"I'm okay," Casey said. "See you later."

Brian hesitated. "Are you sure?" he asked. "I told Ms. Williams I'd check on your ankle."

Watching the deer with him had been so nice that Casey had almost forgotten she was mad at him. As usual, though, he couldn't wait to remind her that he was just doing his job, and she was nothing special to him.

"I *told* you I'm okay," she said. "You don't have to keep checking up on me every minute."

Brian's green eyes darkened, then he looked away and nodded. Without saying another word, he stood up on the pedals and rode quickly away. Casey was so frustrated that she didn't even look up until he was nearly out of sight.

She hadn't meant to sound so obnoxious, but she couldn't help it. Brian was never going to think she was someone special now that she'd made such a fool of herself again. Thinking about it was just too humiliating. She was determined to treat him like everybody else from then on.

As it turned out, she didn't have to worry about it. For the rest of the morning, whenever she saw someone riding toward her, it turned out to be Sue.

By the time Casey rode into lunch camp, the other kids had almost finished eating again. Determined not to look for Brian, she quickly grabbed a sandwich and went to sit with Amy and Tim.

"It's too bad you showed up," Tim said. "I wanted that sandwich."

"I bet," Casey said. "You've probably eaten three already."

"Two and a half," Amy said, holding up half a sandwich. "I made him share the last one with me."

Casey wondered if Tim and Amy were interested in each other. It would be great if they were, she decided, but that was depressing, too. She had spent half the summer preparing for a trip to get together with Brian, while Tim and Amy practically stumbled over each other, and they immediately became a pair.

The same with Greg and Laura, Casey thought. It just didn't seem fair. Everything she had looked forward to on the trip involved Brian Warner. She had imagined sitting around the campfire with him, and riding through the canyon with him, and walking in the woods with him. What she hadn't imagined was that they wouldn't be speaking to each other by the third day of the trip.

"Hey," Amy said, touching her on the shoulder. "I asked if you're going to ride this afternoon?"

"Oh," Casey said. She lifted her foot and wiggled it back and forth for a minute. For the last couple of hours, her ankle had been tired. Now that she and Brian weren't speaking, it seemed more tired than ever. "I don't think so," she said. All the ambition and competitiveness she had felt over the past six weeks seemed to have suddenly drained out of her. "I think I'll go back to camp."

"Great," Tim said. "We're going, too."

"You're kidding," Casey said. "How come?"

Amy grinned. "Because Tim can't take the pressure," she said. "And *I* want to take a shower. Why else?"

Casey wasn't sure whether they were telling the truth or just doing it for her, but she decided not to ask. Having Tim and Amy back at the camp with her would be more fun than hanging around alone. Even though things with Brian weren't going to work out, the trip wasn't a total loss. She had made some new friends. And she had her bike, which she genuinely enjoyed.

Back at camp Amy went to take a shower as

soon as they finished unloading their bikes from the van. "Take your time," Casey said. "Just leave me some hot water."

"There's plenty," Amy called back. "Unless you-know-who has been around."

"For all I know, she could have been," Casey said. "She's always so far ahead of me that I don't even know she's there."

"You and everyone else," Amy said. "I wonder what she's trying to prove."

"She doesn't have to prove anything," Casey said. "She's already *got* everything."

"Except Brian Warner," Amy said. "I think she's got a thing for him."

Casey gulped. She was glad Amy was in the shower where she couldn't see her face. "What makes you think it isn't mutual?" she said. "They're always hanging around together."

"No way," Amy said immediately. "*She's* hanging around. Brian just puts up with her because he's a sweet guy. He's probably the only one here who's nice to her."

Casey remembered Laura saying almost the same thing back when she was trying to meet Brian at the pool. Maybe they were right, but then, why had Brian looked angry at *her* when she told Leslie off? It didn't matter now, anyway. Brian had ruined the trip for her by making a big deal about her ankle. The ankle wasn't that bad, and he should have let her handle it herself.

"What's with you and Tim?" she said, to change the subject. "And don't tell me it's just a coincidence that you both decided to come back to camp."

Amy stepped out of the shower, wrapped in a big white towel. "He's totally wonderful," she said. "I can't believe I never noticed him before."

"I know what you mean," Casey said, thinking about how she had flipped over Brian. Then she saw Amy's curious look and wished she had kept her mouth shut.

But it was too late. "Like you and Brian?" Amy said, grinning from ear to ear.

Casey shrugged. "Maybe," she said. "We all make mistakes sometimes."

Amy finished dressing and started drying her hair with a towel. "The only mistake you're making is the one about Leslie," she said.

Casey shrugged again and dropped her quarters into the hot water meter. She was tired of talking about Brian Warner. She had worked so hard toward this trip to be with him and now it seemed as though their relationship was never going to go anywhere. There was nothing to do now but to enjoy the rest of the trip without him.

Chapter Fourteen

Sunday morning Tim and Amy seemed as though they wanted to be alone, so Casey ate breakfast with Sue. "Seems like rain today," Casey said, looking up at the overcast sky.

Sue ate her last bite of pancakes and nodded. "It better *not* rain today. This is our last full day of riding. We start home at noon tomorrow."

Casey could hardly believe the trip was almost over. The last few days had gone by in seconds, compared to the weeks she'd spent working for them. The next day was Labor Day, and after that came the first day of school.

"I'm going to get some more pancakes," Sue said. "Do you want any?"

"No thanks," Casey said, shaking her head. As soon as Sue left, Ms. Williams came and sat down across from Casey. "I think you'd better not plan on riding today," she said. "You've had trouble with that ankle for two days in a row. If you keep straining it, it could get worse."

"But it's the *last* day," Casey protested. "One more day isn't going to matter. I came here to ride my bike and I'm hardly getting to spend any time on it."

Ms. Williams looked apologetic, but it was obvious that she had already made up her mind. "If you want to ride, we'll have to drive into town and call your parents to ask their permission," she said. "It's too great a risk."

Casey stared down at the table, trying to figure out what to do. There was no point in phoning her parents. They would go along with whatever Ms. Williams said.

"All right," she said at last. "Don't bother calling my parents. I'll just stay in camp all day."

"I'm afraid you'll have to ride along with me this morning," Ms. Williams said. "We need both vans for lunch camp, and I can't leave you here alone."

Casey groaned out loud. As hard as she tried to forget about Brian and have a good time, things kept going from bad to worse. Now she was going to be stuck riding in a van and sitting around with Mr. Ramsey and Ms. Williams. She could just imagine what Laura would say when she got home and told her about it.

When the other kids gathered with their bikes, she walked over to say goodbye to Tim and Amy. "Don't look so down," Amy said. "It's probably going to rain, anyway."

"I'm not so sure," Casey said. "I don't see anyone running for their tents."

Tim glanced up at the clouds. The sky was beginning to clear, but the air still felt heavy and damp. "I hate getting my hair wet," he said. "I'll stay in your tent with you."

"No way," Amy said, grabbing him by the arm. "I'm not lending you out to Casey until after lunch."

Casey laughed, but seeing them having fun together made her more depressed than ever. "See you later," she said and went to climb into the van with Ms. Williams.

As Ms. Williams steered the van onto the road, she told Casey they would drive to the first checkpoint and wait there until everyone was accounted for. After that, they would go on to the lunch camp and start setting things up.

Staring out the window, Casey thought about her disastrous trip. The minute she had seen Leslie in Brian's van back at the school yard, she should have known everything would go

159

wrong. Having an injured ankle was frustrating, but it wouldn't have kept her from having fun. At least, not if things had turned out the way she had planned, and being stuck with Ms. Williams was the final straw.

That was *before* she saw Brian come riding into lunch camp right behind Leslie. "Thanks, Brian," she heard Leslie say. "I don't know what I would have done if you hadn't helped me work that cramp out of my leg."

"It's okay," Brian said as he loosened the strap on his helmet. Casey waited for him to add, "It's my job," the way he always did with her. Instead, he walked over to get a sandwich and a cup of juice. Amy was wrong, Casey decided. Brian wasn't just being nice to Leslie because she had no other friends on the trip. There had to be more to it.

After that, she was so miserable that she could hardly keep from crying. On the way back to the main camp, Ms. Williams kept giving her concerned looks. "I know how you must feel," she said after a while. "It can't be much fun finding yourself grounded for most of the trip."

The sympathetic way she said it was too much. Casey burst into tears. "I don't know why everyone is making such a big deal about my ankle," she sobbed. "If Brian Warner had just kept his mouth shut, I could be riding my bike."

When they got back to camp, Ms. Williams put her arm around Casey's shoulders and smiled. "I can understand your being upset," she said. "But you're not being fair to Brian. Joint injuries can be a serious problem, even for professional athletes. If you keep straining them, they might never heal properly. Instead of blowing up at Brian, you should have thanked him for looking out for you."

It was all Casey could do not to burst into tears again. "I don't have a joint injury," she said. "I just twisted my ankle."

Ms. Williams shook her head. "We don't know that, Casey. Until you've had it checked out, it's foolish to take chances. Brian knows that. It was big of him to behave responsibly, even though he knew you weren't going to like it."

Suddenly Casey was so confused that she didn't know what to think. Maybe Ms. Williams was right. Instead of getting mad at Brian, she should have realized he was looking out for her. She probably *would* have realized it, if she hadn't been so jealous of Leslie Duncan.

It was crazy the way she had been getting so worked up about everything lately when she used to be so relaxed. Casey had been so caught up in getting what she wanted that summer that she had forgotten to think about anything else. Being ambitious might be fine for some people, but all it had gotten her was trouble.

When the other kids came back to camp that afternoon, Casey still hadn't sorted everything out. The one thing she was sure of was that Brian *was* a nice guy. Even though he hadn't fallen madly in love with her, he had helped her a lot. Maybe he *was* only doing his job, but he was looking out for her.

And knowing that made her feel worse than ever. She had never been good at apologizing. Now, she was going to have to do it again.

The trouble was, every time she got up the nerve to go over and talk to him, someone else got there first. It was almost as if she were back at the swimming pool, when she had first started trying to talk to him. But, now, it was even worse. She couldn't just walk up to him and start pouring her heart out in front of everyone.

At last, she found a chance to be alone with him after dinner. It was twilight, and most of the kids were gathered around the fire, celebrating the last night of the trip. Brian seemed particularly quiet. After a while he stood up and walked to the edge of the campground. He looked into the shadowy woods for a minute, then sat down alone on a log bench.

It's now or never, Casey told herself. She got

up quietly and went over and sat down beside him. "Hi," she said.

Brian was leaning forward, with his elbows on his knees, twisting a twig between his fingers. He glanced up and said, "Hi," then looked back at the twig.

When he looked away from her, Casey's heart sank. "It was nice of you to be so concerned about my ankle," she heard herself say. "I'm sorry I acted like such a baby."

The words seemed to come from someone else's voice. Much to Casey's surprise, Brian actually looked relieved.

"I know the trip hasn't been much fun for you," he said. "I shouldn't have let you come with that ankle in the first place."

"It isn't your fault," Casey said. "I was the one who didn't want to tell anyone about my ankle."

Brian kept fidgeting with the twig, then snapped it in two and dropped it. "But I *knew* you were going to have trouble with it," he said. "I was just being selfish. I wanted you to come because it would be more fun for *me*. I should have realized it would be a drag for you. I wouldn't blame you if you never wanted to speak to me again."

Casey couldn't believe her ears. "*Me* speak to

you!" she said. "I thought you weren't speaking to me."

Brian looked at her in astonishment. "Why wouldn't I speak to you?"

"Because—because—oh, never mind." Casey laughed. "I think I got a few things mixed up."

Casey thought she finally understood Brian Warner. He was confident about his athletic ability, but when it came to relationships, he was no more sure of himself than she was.

"I worked all summer for this trip," she admitted, "just so I could get a chance to see you without—"

Just then she heard footsteps and looked up and saw Leslie Duncan walking toward them. "Hi, Brian," Leslie said. "I was wondering if you could take a look at my front brakes before it gets dark."

Casey held her breath, waiting to see what would happen. Brian shook his head. "Sorry," he told Leslie. "I'm busy right now. Could you ask someone else?"

Casey was so astonished that she nearly gasped. Then she caught her breath again, waiting for Leslie to object. For some reason Leslie just stared at them for a minute, then turned and walked away.

"I always thought you liked *her*," Casey said, still surprised.

"Leslie's nice and all, but she's much too competitive for me. I've wanted to get to know *you* ever since that poli-sci class," he said. "You just never seemed interested in me."

Suddenly Casey and Brian were looking into each other's eyes and smiling. The next thing she knew, he was leaning toward her and kissing her gently on the lips. Feeling as though she were in a dream, Casey put her arms around his neck and kissed him back.

"All of a sudden, I'm glad I came on the trip," she whispered.

Brian grinned, and Casey could see golden sparks in his green eyes. "That's what I like about you," he said. "You're so easygoing about things."

"I'm not as easygoing as people think," Casey said. "If I were, I wouldn't even be here right now."

Brian looked into her eyes for a moment, then kissed the tip of her nose. "In that case," he said, "I'm glad you've decided to become ambitious."

Darkness was settling around the edge of the camp. They walked back to the campfire and stood around talking to some of the other kids. Leslie kept glancing at them. Casey felt awkward and excited at the same time. She was glad Brian was holding *her* hand and not

Leslie's. But, somehow, she didn't feel like rubbing it in anymore.

After a few more hours of talking, and toasting marshmallows around the crackling campfire, Mr. Ramsey said, "Okay. Let's put out the fire and turn in." Brian walked Casey to her tent and kissed her good night. As soon as he was gone, Amy burst into the tent, grinning as though she had just been elected prom queen. "I told you you were wrong," she said. "Tell me everything."

Casey grinned back at her and shrugged. "There's nothing to tell," she said.

Before Amy could ask any more questions, Sue came dashing in. "It's about time," she said. "The whole camp has been wondering when you two were going to get it together."

Suddenly Casey realized she was blushing. It was incredible that it had been so obvious to everyone but her and Brian. It was even more incredible that he'd actually kissed her! Incredible and wonderful. She lay on her cot thinking about it until she finally drifted off to sleep.

It was hard to believe that the trip was over. Back at home, Casey wheeled her bicycle into the garage and stood looking at its gleaming red paint. She thought about what a wreck the bike had been when she bought it, and a smile spread across her face.

Then she heard footsteps outside and turned to see Brian come into the garage, carrying her sleeping bag and outdoor bag. He dropped her gear beside the door and came over and put one arm around her shoulders.

Casey turned to look up into his eyes. She felt as though she could look into them forever. Then he dipped his head to kiss her lightly on the lips, and she closed her eyes and wrapped her arms around him.

"I hope I'm going to be seeing a lot of you this year," Brian said softly.

"Me, too," Casey said, snuggling her head under his chin. Laura had been right, she thought. It had been a weird summer—getting a job, quarreling with Laura, fixing the bike, and competing with Leslie Duncan. But now everything had fallen into place. "I can't believe summer is over," she whispered. "It seems as though it should just be starting."

Brian held her for a moment, then put his hand under her chin and tilted her face up so that he could look into her eyes. "It's just starting," he said. "And I have a feeling it's going to be all downhill coasting from here on."

His face broke into a smile, and Casey grinned

back at him. "I hope you're right," she said jokingly. "I'm not crazy about riding uphill."

"I noticed," Brian said with a grin. "But I never saw anyone who tried so hard."

"Are you laughing at me?" Casey demanded, trying to look indignant.

"A little," he admitted. And before she could protest, he folded her into his arms.

They walked out of the garage, holding hands. Casey paused at the door to look back at her bike. The Challenger had been a good investment. It had carried her through the whole crazy summer, right into Brian's arms.

We hope you enjoyed reading this book. If you would like to receive further information about titles available in the Bantam series, just write to the address below, with your name and address:

Kim Prior
Bantam Books
61–63 Uxbridge Road
Ealing
London W5 5SA

If you live in Australia or New Zealand and would like more information about the series, please write to:

Sally Porter
Transworld Publishers (Aust.) Pty. Ltd.
15–23 Helles Avenue
Moorebank
N.S.W. 2170
AUSTRALIA

Kiri Martin
Transworld Publishers (N.Z.) Ltd.
Cnr. Moselle and Waipareira Avenues
Henderson
Auckland
NEW ZEALAND

All Bantam Young Adult books are available at your bookshop or newsagent, or can be ordered from the following address:

Corgi/Bantam Books
Cash Sales Department
PO Box 11
Falmouth
Cornwall
TR10 9EN

Please list the title(s) you would like, and send together with a cheque or postal order. You should allow for the cost of the book(s) plus postage and packing charges as follows:

All orders up to a total of £5.00   50p
All orders in excess of £5.00   Free

Please note that payment must be made in pounds sterling; other currencies are unacceptable.

(The above applies to readers in the UK and Republic of Ireland only)

B.F.P.O. customers, please allow for the cost of the book(s) plus the following for postage and packing: 60p for the first book, 25p for the second book and 15p per copy for the next 7 books, thereafter 9p per book.

Overseas customers, please allow £1.25 for postage and packing for the first book, 75p for the second book, and 28p for each subsequent title ordered.

Thank you!

Janet Quin-Harkin's Sugar & Spice

Watch out for a smashing new series from the best-selling author, Janet Quin-Harkin.

Meet the most unlikely pair of best friends since Toni and Jill from Janet Quin-Harkin's TEN BOY SUMMER.

Caroline's thrilled to find out she's got a long-lost cousin exactly her age. But she's horrified when Chrissy comes to spend a year with her family. Caroline's a reserved and polite only child – now she has to share her life with a loud, unsophisticated, embarrassing farm girl!

Coming soon – wherever Bantam paperbacks are sold!